William had been working in this field for more than six hours. The overhead sun beat down upon his back, and sweat made his shirt stick to his skin.

He lowered his hoe to the ground and leaned his full weight on the farm tool. Reaching into his back pocket, he grabbed his handkerchief and swiped it across his brow then down his face. Without the benefit of a looking glass, he had no idea if he managed to rid himself of the dirt and grime. But it had to be far better than he looked a moment before.

Then he saw her. A brown-haired young woman moving from worker to worker, carrying a pail of water with a dipper. Perfect. The last thing he wanted was another benevolent society member reminding him of where he'd been before the panic and all that he'd lost. Fresh water sounded good. He just didn't want it to come from someone like her. Yet here she was, headed in their direction.

William glanced down at Jacob, who worked alongside him. At least for his brother's sake, he'd remain cordial. But he didn't have to like it.

AMBER STOCKTON is a freelance Web designer and author whose articles and short stories have appeared in local, national, and international publications. Her writing career began as a columnist for her high school and college newspapers. Her first publication in a book appeared in the form of nine contributions (as a single!) to *101 Ways to Romance Your Marriage* by Debra White Smith. She learned to read at age three and hasn't put down books since. A member of ACFW (American Christian Fiction Writers), she lives with her husband and fellow writer, Stuart, and their new baby girl in beautiful Colorado. Visit her Web site to learn more or to contact her: www.amberstockton.com.

Hearts and Harvest

Amber Stockton

Heartsong Presents

My heartfelt thanks go first to my husband for not letting me get away with any excuses. Thanks also to my family on both sides, my editors (JoAnne, April, and Rachel), and to my local crit group for their honest critiques. I couldn't write my books without all of you!

A note from the Author:
I love to hear from my readers! You may correspond with me by writing:

Amber Stockton
Author Relations
PO Box 721
Uhrichsville, OH 44683

ISBN 978-1-60260-576-3

HEARTS AND HARVEST

All scripture quotations are taken from the King James Version of the Bible.

All of the characters and events in this book are fictitious. Any resemblance to actual persons, living or dead, or to actual events is purely coincidental.

Our mission is to publish and distribute inspirational products offering exceptional value and biblical encouragement to the masses.

PRINTED IN THE U.S.A.

one

"And remember," Pastor Owens said loudly and clearly as he concluded his sermon, "we have placed boxes at the back by the doors for any donations you wish to make on behalf of those who are now farming the public lands in order to provide for their families."

Annabelle Lawson fixed her eyes on the pastor. His crisp, pressed purple robe with gold accents flowed in tandem with his motions as he made a sweeping gesture out over those gathered. The compassion in his light brown eyes only added to his youthful appearance, despite the traces of gray she caught at his temples.

He always looked out for those less fortunate, but never before had his plea compelled her to contribute like it had today.

"Some of you have donated pieces of your land for farming, and I know these families appreciate your generosity. But for those who are unable to do that, you can contribute through the donation boxes. Every bit you give will go toward purchasing farming tools and equipment for these families."

Had Father been one of those the pastor mentioned as having donated land? They certainly had enough to spare. She'd ask him after the service ended.

"And now go in peace and in the knowledge of our heavenly Father's love."

With that the assemblage stood almost in unison, and Annabelle paused as individuals made their way en masse toward the back.

She clutched her handbag in one hand and held her Bible to her chest as she slipped from her family's pew after her parents and entered the center aisle. Her younger brother and sister followed. She stepped aside to let them pass then glanced toward the front of the church at the elaborate furnishings and ornate fixtures, from the hanging chandeliers to the brass candelabras. Marble tabletops sat on hand-carved wooden stands, and rich burgundy carpet adorned the steps as well as the floor of the elevated dais from which the pastor gave his sermon.

That was where the evidence of affluence ended. Annabelle observed the worn pews in great need of whitewashing or a new coat of paint. It almost felt as if a line divided the church from where the congregation sat and where the pastor stood. The people around her wore clothing in a wide variety of quality and style. Here status didn't matter. Even the pastor, in all of his finery, possessed a welcoming personality that embraced everyone equally.

Annabelle again looked at the wide array of appearances in the attendees. How could her family and many who attended this church have so much when others who joined them had so little?

The financial crisis last year had struck in a random pattern. Thanks to the poor investment choices and risky building decisions by the railroad companies, financing had been lost and banks had run out of money. Both the rich and the poor had been affected. Young and old. Businessman and tradesman alike. Annabelle volunteered for one of Detroit's charity services, and her supervisor had recently confided to her that their stores and funds were either depleted or quite low. They had little to give to those in need.

This idea from Pastor Owens could help all the city's charities. And in turn the families could maintain their pride or self-respect as they farmed on their own without accepting handouts. Donations alone wouldn't help. Paving the way for those who had lost much to be able to work would bring fortune to all.

"Annabelle, dear. Don't dawdle." Her mother's voice called to her from a few pews away. "Katie will have Sunday dinner ready by the time we get home. We haven't a moment to spare."

"Yes, Mother."

After a final glance around the haven the church provided, Annabelle made her way to the back. As she passed the boxes, her conscience pricked her rather soundly. Seeing the departing backs of her family, she knew she must hurry. Service had run later than normal. A full half hour, in fact. Without further thought, she reached into her handbag and withdrew all the coins she had. She dropped the money in the slotted box and smiled at the sound of it joining the other money already donated. It wasn't much, but it felt good to help.

"Annabelle!"

The sharp yet soft reprimand made Annabelle start. She looked up to see her mother peering around the doorframe, an impatient expression on her face. If Mother had been standing inside, her foot no doubt would have been tapping against the stone floor. Felicity Lawson normally maintained a cool demeanor. But everyone had his or her limits. No sense making Mother any more upset.

"Coming, Mother."

❧

An hour later the Lawson family gathered around the table. Annabelle picked at her plate while the rest of her family devoured the delicious fried chicken, potatoes and gravy, and canned vegetables from their garden. She didn't want to insult Katie, but she couldn't find much of an appetite.

She stared at how much food they had. Her thoughts wandered to those families going without today. Somehow even Katie's best recipe failed to tempt her taste buds.

"What's the matter, Annabelle?" Her younger brother, Matthew, gave her a poke in the ribs, his voice taking on a taunting tone. "Trying to maintain your graceful figure so some poor, unsuspecting bloke will fall prey to your charms?"

"Matthew! That's enough."

Father's reprimand made her brother straighten in his chair and dip his chin. Brandt Lawson had mediated their little squabbles more times than Annabelle could count. Yet Matthew persisted. The rather tall rascal might be nearing eighteen, but at times he acted like a ten-year-old.

"Sorry, Father."

"It's not me to whom you owe an apology."

"Sorry, Annabelle," he mumbled, not even bothering to look her way.

Annabelle pressed her lips together to hold back a grin, but Father caught her eye and winked. That made her struggle even harder. Father knew what it was like to have a younger brother. Uncle Charles always seemed to be looking for his next victim, and Father had told her he hadn't changed a bit since they were boys. It looked as if Matthew had inherited that streak of mischief from their uncle.

"Now, Annabelle," Father continued in a more congenial tone. "Is there something wrong with the food? Or do you have something else on your mind that's keeping you from eating?"

She set down her fork and reached for her water glass. After taking a drink, she lowered the glass and looked to her left where Father sat waiting for an answer.

"It's not the food, Father. Katie should again be praised for her efforts."

"Then what is it, dear?"

Annabelle glanced at Mother from the corner of her eye. Matthew and their younger sister, Victoria, also waited expectantly. She hadn't meant to interrupt their meal. But now that she had their attention, she'd better take full advantage. Returning her gaze to Father, she attempted to formulate her conflicting thoughts into words.

"This morning. At church. Pastor Owens spoke of the families in need of assistance and mentioned the vacant plots of land being donated for farming use."

"Yes." Mother sighed. "It is difficult to see so many in such dire need. We ourselves aren't without feeling the effects of the crisis, but we fared much better than most, thanks to your father's well-spread investments." Mother looked down the table at Father, and the two shared a silent bond.

"Exactly," Annabelle continued. "And don't misunderstand me. I'm grateful that we were spared for the most part, but somehow thanking God for our abundance feels wrong in light of those we know who have nothing."

"What do you propose we do about that, Annabelle?" Father steepled his fingers and rested his forearms on the edge of the table. "We can't exactly give everything we have in surplus and place ourselves on equal footing with them."

"Nor do I expect us to, Father. I merely wanted to say how inspired I was by Pastor Owens's sermon. The Bible commands us to help our neighbors, and what we do unto the least of them, we do as unto Christ."

Victoria leaned forward. "I put my coins in the box today, Annabelle. Did you?"

Annabelle looked across the table at her sister. Even at twelve she possessed a heart of gold.

"Yes, I did. Everything I had with me."

At times Annabelle felt as if she came in second place to her sister where charity was concerned. Whatever her family did, Victoria was certain to be as involved as possible.

"But I feel we can do more. I just don't know what."

Silence fell upon the table, and her family all wore introspective expressions. Several moments passed. Finally, Father cleared his throat, and all eyes turned toward him.

"Well, I was going to wait until later to announce this, but I suppose now is as good a time as any."

He paused, and Annabelle turned her head to look at Mother, who nodded with a smile. They had done something. Now she was anxious to find out what.

"Following our good mayor's lead of sacrifice, I've put up that vacant plot we own on Marshall to be used for farming. It neighbors several other vacant plots that have also been donated. I gather it will bring about a sizable profit for our city and those in need."

Annabelle clapped her hands and beamed a smile at him. "Oh, Father! That's wonderful. When I heard Pastor Owens this morning mention the need for land, I wanted to ask if we had any to give. When did you donate it? How much land is it? When will the workers arrive to start working? I want to be there to help in any way I can."

The deep sound of Father's chuckle rumbled from his end of the table. "Slow down, Annabelle. I only just spoke with the mayor last week. I daresay it will be another week or more before any families are assigned to our particular plot." He raised a hand, palm out, in her direction. "But I promise to notify you the moment I hear anything further."

"I want to help as well, Father."

"You will, Victoria. You will."

"Father," Matthew inserted, "didn't Mayor Pingree sell his thoroughbred horse and give the proceeds to the farming fund?"

Father nodded. "Yes, he did. Where did you hear about that?"

Matthew shrugged. "Oh, some of the young men at the

copper refinery were talking about it the other day at work. I overheard one of them say it and wondered if they were exaggerating or not."

"It is true. And his act of goodwill encouraged many others to follow suit. Now we have a substantial fund for farming equipment, and we should be able to provide these families with everything they need to get started."

Annabelle listened as Father continued to lay out what he knew would be the plan once the farming commenced. Just this morning she had wanted to get involved and help. Little did she know how close the opportunity would come to her own home. Now she could fulfill God's commandment and at the same time feel satisfied in what she had to offer. Excitement built inside her.

She could hardly wait to get started.

ಋ

William Berringer trudged behind his father as they approached the barren plot of land that would become their place of work for several months, possibly even years. The abandoned factory building at the far edge of the land would house several families working this plot. He sighed. How in the world had something like this happened to them?

One day they were living a comfortable life with plenty to eat and had more than enough money to afford the finer things if they wanted them. The next, their stronghold had crumbled, they had lost their home, and the jobs he and his father held had been stripped away. All because of railroad overbuilding and shaky railroad financing that set off a series of bank failures.

If it hadn't been for the bankruptcy of Philadelphia and Reading Railroad last year, concern over the economy might not have worsened. But it did, and people rushed to with-draw their money from banks. In no time at all, gold and silver reserves were depleted and the value of the dollar had decreased. Their life savings disappeared, and they couldn't meet their mortgage obligations. Everything they had invested was gone. William almost didn't want to blink for fear that something even more disastrous would occur.

"Well, here we are." His father gestured with a wide sweep of his arm. "Our source of income for as long as it takes until we can rebuild what we've lost."

And that could take years if they only had farming as an option. William sneered at the weed-covered ground. Gusts of wind stirred the loose dirt from a bare patch nearby and created a tiny swirl around them. Maybe he could get caught up in one and be taken far away from here. Far away from the gloomy prospect of what the financial crisis had done to him and his family.

"At least we know we aren't alone," his mother chimed in. Her forced cheerfulness was almost too much. "Many others—friends and neighbors—are suffering the same fate. If they can do this, so can we."

Father stepped close and wrapped his arm around his wife. "You are absolutely right, my dear. It might not be much, but our God has provided."

"God?" William couldn't help the derision that filled his voice. "You talk of God?" He swung out his arm in a sweeping gesture over the land in front of them. "Where was God when the crisis occurred? Where was He when we were forced from our home? Where was He when we lost everything?"

Jacob, his little brother, looked up at all three of them in silence. He moved his gaze from one to another, curiosity and uncertainty reflected in his eyes.

"God is right where He's always been, my boy," Father replied. "With us." Daniel Berringer was nothing if not forthright and stalwart. He led their family with a strength and determination William admired and hoped to have himself one day.

But that strength wasn't what he wanted right now. He wanted answers. He wanted solutions. He wanted a guarantee that this new lot in life would turn out to be a prosperous venture and that they could return to the life they once knew before too long. From what he could see, the likelihood of that seemed as distant as the grouping of various land plots that stretched out to the north and west of the city.

"Well, if God's been right here all along, then He wanted this to happen to us. And if that's the case, I want to know why."

Lucille Berringer came and placed a gentle hand on William's shoulder. "Sometimes, William, we aren't able to ask why. We simply must obey and do the best with what we've been given."

William fought hard not to shrug off his mother's touch. She meant well, but he wasn't in the mood for comfort. "I thought we *had* done the best we could. *Before* all this happened. Father and I had good jobs in finance and industry and had established what we thought was a rather solid family business. I was also looking to expand into manufacturing with some of Thomas Edison's ventures. We worked hard and remained faithful with the fruits of our labors. Was it not good enough to suit God?"

"That's enough, William!" Father's voice took on a hard edge—one William knew brooked no argument.

Jacob's eyes widened, and William regretted his previous words. The last thing he wanted to do was cause Jacob to become bitter. His brother didn't deserve this, either. At least he was young, though. He had his whole life ahead of him. William, on the other hand, had been making plans to move from apprenticeship to management when the crisis struck. He should be furthering his own career right now. He should be courting young ladies and thinking about starting his own family.

Father clenched his fists at his side, then relaxed them. "I realize how difficult this is for you. It's difficult for all of us. We have all lost a great deal. But I will not have you allowing your anger at the situation to poison the hope we have, thanks to a generous donor who has given us this land. There are many others who have not been as fortunate, some who even now are headed west with nothing left here in the city." A sigh, full of acceptance, blew forth from his lips. "You would do well to remember that."

William lowered his head. Father was right. His best friend growing up had done just that. Unable to see any hope in Detroit or any of the areas nearby, Ben's family had packed up and headed west toward Seattle or Portland. Others went to Denver or Salt Lake City or even San Francisco. Anywhere but here. For a moment William wished his family had followed. But no guarantees existed there, either. So for now at least they had a roof over their heads—drafty and run-down though it was—and the opportunity to grow food. He might as well make the best of it.

"I'm sorry, Father. I know we're not the only ones who are suffering. I'll try not to be so negative."

Father's expression softened and relief spread across his face. "Thank you."

Mother gave his shoulder a squeeze before once again stepping to her husband's side. William looked down at Jacob and smiled. The lad put his hand in William's and grinned. William reached out and tousled his brother's hair. At least they hadn't lost each other. Other families he knew hadn't been as fortunate.

❧

William had been working in this field for more than six hours. The overhead sun beat down upon his back, and sweat made his shirt stick to his skin.

He lowered his hoe to the ground and leaned his full weight on the farm tool. Reaching into his back pocket, he grabbed his handkerchief and swiped it across his brow then down his face. Without the benefit of a looking glass, he had no idea if he managed to rid himself of the dirt and grime. But it had to be far better than he looked a moment before.

Then he saw her. A brown-haired young woman moving from worker to worker, carrying a pail of water with a dipper. Perfect. The last thing he wanted was another benevolent society member reminding him of where he'd been before the panic and all that he'd lost. Fresh water sounded good. He just didn't want it to come from someone like her. Yet here she was, headed in their direction.

William glanced down at Jacob, who worked alongside him. At least for his brother's sake, he'd remain cordial. But he didn't have to like it.

two

"Thank you." William accepted the dipper and took a long drink. The liquid quenched his thirst and cooled his over-heated body. Immediate relief filled his limbs and made him feel as if he could work another ten hours.

"You are quite welcome," she replied. "I can imagine how difficult it is to spend so many hours in the sun. Would that I could offer more than just water."

What about some financial assistance or a job other than farming? William asked the question in his mind, but he didn't speak it aloud. "The water is enough. Thank you."

The young woman dipped her chin in acknowledgment and bent to offer the pail to his younger brother. Jacob hesitated and looked at William, as if seeking permission or asking if it was all right. Before William could respond, the woman set down the water and knelt in a dry patch of dirt, puffs exploding around her. She didn't seem too concerned that her well-pressed skirts were getting soiled or that her styled hair had fallen into slight disarray, though. Instead, she focused her entire attention on Jacob as she reached out to touch his shoulder. Jacob startled, but his attention went straight to the young woman. She smiled and held out the dipper again.

"Don't worry. You can have as much as you like. There is plenty here for everyone."

William watched the transformation on his brother's face. The lad went from uncertain to eager in a matter of seconds. He reached out a grubby hand and took the dipper, guzzling its contents in one gulp. Melodious laughter bubbled from the young woman's lips as she filled the dipper again and held it out to Jacob, who accepted more without hesitation.

For weeks Jacob had worked hard and done his part. He had dug in with gusto, never once complaining and always right there by William's side. The only concern William and his parents had was Jacob's lack of interest in people. He no longer sought out other lads his age, and when anyone approached, he held back and attempted to disappear. He didn't speak to anyone but his family.

Today, however, was different. This young woman managed to coax a reaction from Jacob—quite a feat in and of itself. Her attentiveness and soft-spoken words must have gotten through to Jacob. Perhaps William had been wrong to make such a hasty judgment of her. And those beguiling blue eyes paired with the kind smile made him want to get to know her better.

She had already served his parents. Jacob was the last of his family. If William didn't do or say something, she would leave them and move to the next family. He had to keep her here, even for just a few extra moments.

"His name's Jacob."

The woman rocked back on her heels, then stood in one slow, fluid motion, coming about seven inches below his six-foot height. Not a drop of water sloshed from the pail. Hooking the dipper on the edge, she extended her free hand toward Jacob. William widened his eyes and raised his eyebrows. Jacob showed his surprise as well, his expression no doubt mirroring William's. A rather bold move on her part. Young women never offered a hand to anyone they met. Maybe she was making an exception for Jacob.

"My name is Annabelle Lawson. Pleased to meet you, Jacob. You may call me Miss Annabelle."

Again his brother glanced up at him. He gave a sharp nod. Jacob reached out and struck hands with the young woman.

"Nice to meet you, too, Miss Annabelle."

Annabelle. The name suited her. William searched his memory and years of study for the Latin origin. *Graceful.* Yes, she had been named well. In fact, William felt rather awkward in her presence. He'd never had a problem speaking with the fairer gender before. But standing in his oversized breeches that felt like coarse burlap, the loose-fitting shirt in need of washing, worn and dirty shoes, and a ragged cap, he lacked the confidence he normally possessed. His previous wardrobe contained nothing appropriate for working the fields, so he'd been forced to resort to handouts from some of the charitable donations. Good thing his brother seemed to hold her interest for now. He certainly didn't feel ready to venture into conversation at the moment.

"And how old are you, young Jacob?" Annabelle released Jacob's hand only to tap the edge of the boy's cap.

Jacob warmed to her immediately. Puffing out his chest and snapping his suspenders, he rocked back and forth on his heels and beamed a wide smile. "I'm eight."

"Well, now, you're quite a grown-up young man already. Your parents are no doubt proud to have you working alongside them. I would surmise that you probably do the work of two young lads your age."

William chuckled at the image his brother presented. If Jacob's chest got any bigger, he'd explode with all the proud air he'd inhaled. But William was impressed with how quickly Annabelle had set his brother at ease. Jacob could be the inquisitive sort, but since they'd lost everything, his demeanor had dampened in a substantial way. William gave his brother a pat on the back, which caused Jacob to relax and release the breath he'd been holding.

"And how about you?" Annabelle switched her attention from Jacob to him. "Do you have a name as well?"

William opened his mouth to speak, but no sound came

out. Despite the water he'd drunk a few moments ago, his mouth felt as dry as the ground he now dug would be in summer. He swallowed several times and attempted to bring moisture back to his tongue. Before he could speak, though, Jacob chimed in.

"His name's William. William Berringer. And he's my brother."

Amusement danced across Annabelle's face. She no doubt thought him quite the fool for not being able to answer for himself. "William and Jacob Berringer. Such fine, strong names. Your father and mother chose well."

William cleared his throat and managed to croak, "Thank you."

Great. Was that all he could say to this young woman? It was the third time he'd uttered those words in almost as many minutes. She might believe him a half-wit with a limited vocabulary if he didn't figure out how to get his tongue and head to work in tandem instead of fighting with each other.

He tried again. "How did you come to be distributing water at this farm plot? You're the first nonworker I've seen around here in days."

Annabelle looked away. William thought he saw a hint of pink steal into her cheeks. But she composed herself and returned his gaze. "This land belongs to my father. He donated it to help with this crisis. I learned of it two weeks ago and was eager to help in any way that I could. But Father forbade me to come unaccompanied, so I had to wait until he made his weekly visit before I could venture over this way."

"You mean you own all this land?" Jacob swung his arms wide and spun in a circle as he gestured toward the expansive plot where at least six families farmed. "You must be rich!"

"Jacob!" William scolded.

His brother ducked his head and scuffed the worn toe of his shoe in the dirt. "Sorry," he mumbled.

It was bad enough their family had been reduced to this type of work. They didn't need to act like the migrant workers they were and present the appearance of discourteous behavior as well.

Annabelle didn't seem to mind, though. The soft smile on her lips and twinkle in her eyes proved that. "Your apology is accepted, Jacob, but I would still like to answer your question, if I may."

She looked to William to obtain silent permission. Amazed at her forthrightness and the fact that she had no qualms about speaking with them, he could only nod.

"My father has made some very wise decisions over the years. But that doesn't mean our family is better than anyone else. We might be rich compared to some, but that could all change. In fact, that's why I've come to help. It could be me and my family here instead of yours."

"We used to be rich, too. But now we're not."

"Jacob," William warned, keeping his voice low.

Annabelle stayed his protest with her hand. "It's quite all right, Mr. Berringer. As my mother has quoted many times, 'Out of the mouths of babes.' A lot has happened in recent months. This past year has been rather difficult for everyone. Your brother is merely saying what so many are feeling."

"Well, I appreciate your understanding, Miss Lawson. And you can call me William. We might as well dispense with the formalities around here. We aren't exactly being presented at court."

The young woman tilted her head and regarded him with a curious expression. She pressed her lips in a line for a moment then smiled. He thought she might agree. "No, I don't believe we are. . .Mr. Berringer. However, we have only just met, and it wouldn't be proper." Obviously not.

William nodded. "Miss Lawson it is, then."

"Why do I have to call you Miss Annabelle?" His brother

crossed his arms over his chest.

William gave Jacob a playful punch. "Calling her Miss Annabelle is a sign of respect."

"But don't you respect her?"

Heat rushed to William's face, and for once he was grateful for the hot sun that had already made his face a bit red. It seemed his brother had found his precociousness again.

Annabelle's laughter set William's mind at ease. She leaned down so she was almost at eye level with Jacob and smiled. "I'll make you a deal. When you are old enough to own your own piece of land, you may drop the 'Miss' and just call me Annabelle. All right?"

So she was giving Jacob permission to be informal yet insisted William abide by society's dictates? William recalled some from his younger days who had allowed him to address them in a similar fashion, but this was different. Why did William feel as if he'd picked the shorter straw?

Jacob scrunched his face and was silent for several moments as he pondered her offer. Then a grin split his lips, and he stuck out his hand. "Deal."

Annabelle struck hands with him again. "Deal," she repeated.

William thought about how long it would be before that time came to his little brother's life. He hoped by then they would have figured out how to regain their standing in society once again. Right now that possibility seemed too far away to even fathom.

And what about Annabelle? Jacob was sure to remember and hold her to her promise. Would she even be around? Would she even care?

Wait a minute. What was he thinking? He had no business contemplating his future and wondering if she would be in it. He shouldn't even be taking up so much of her time right now. She was here to bring water to everyone, not just him and Jacob. He should step aside and allow her to continue on her way.

"So do you have any other brothers or a sister perhaps?" Annabelle again faced him. "Or is it just the two of you?"

She didn't seem in any hurry to leave, but more families needed water. Who was he to monopolize so much of her time when he was nothing more than a dirt farmer with no land or possessions to call his own?

"Don't you think you should see who else might need some of the water you're offering?" William cringed at how abrupt that sounded. He tried to soften it somehow. "I'm sure there are others who would appreciate it as much as we."

Annabelle hesitated, a mixture of hurt and uncertainty crossing her features. She looked between Jacob and him and back again. Finally, she nodded. Schooling her expression into one of nonchalance, she grasped hold of the bucket and dipper and took one step away.

"Very well. I shall see to the other families. Thank you for taking the time to introduce yourself and speak with me for a few moments. I am certain our paths will cross again."

"Good-bye, Miss Annabelle!" Jacob called to her retreating back.

She pivoted and gave him a soft smile. "Good-bye, Jacob. You behave yourself."

With a final glance at William, she was gone.

William closed his eyes and clenched his teeth. What a fool he'd been. She was only attempting to bestow some kindness on him and his family, and he'd run her off. If what she'd said were true, it would be another week before he'd see her again. That gave her plenty of time to devise a reason to avoid this area of her father's land. She might even decide to send someone else in her place.

At least Jacob had made a good impression. Maybe that was enough to bring her back. William hoped so. Otherwise he'd blown his only opportunity.

❧

Annabelle resisted the urge to turn around again and watch the two brothers. The abrupt change in William's demeanor couldn't have shocked her more had she been splashed in the face with the very water she carried. She could see the tumult of emotions warring within the young man the moment she approached. At first he looked like he would dismiss her and tell her to go back to where she came from.

His desire for the water she brought superseded whatever thoughts he might have had to turn his back on her, though. And despite obvious reservations, he remained cordial. It wasn't until she spoke to his brother that William warmed a little.

She understood his protectiveness. She'd do the same for Victoria in an instant. It was his mannerisms and choice of words that replayed in her mind.

"*. . .dispense with the formalities. . .presented at court. . .*"

He spoke as one whose normal life involved expectations and activities such as those. Considering how widespread the effects of the panic were, the Berringer family could have once been equal or greater in station than she. William might not wear the clothes of other gentleman she knew and his face might be smudged with the evidence of his hard labor, but she knew a true gentleman when she saw one.

And William was it.

In fact, his mannerisms fell second only to the appeal of his nervous behavior and rather boyish charm. It seemed almost comical on a man who stood nearly six feet tall and possessed a build familiar with some form of hard work. With his sandy-colored hair that blew in the breeze and fell in stubborn locks across his forehead, the slight tilt of his mouth when he grinned, and the deep chocolate eyes, he possessed a number of charming qualities. The dimple in his cheek only heightened the attraction. He and his brother had been the first to engage her in any way. The rest of the workers gave her nothing more than a cursory nod as they accepted the water. Some averted their eyes, while others appeared to sneer as if she chose to be here in order to flaunt her superiority or make a mockery of them. That couldn't be further from the truth. Yet knowing that and living with the reality were two entirely different things.

As she finished making her rounds, Annabelle felt compelled to return and continue their conversation. What good would that do? He'd made it clear he didn't want to spend any more time with her. And he did have work to do. If she interfered, it would only make matters worse. No, she'd have to wait until next week. Perhaps by then William would be in a better mood.

"Annabelle!" Father called from one of the supply stations nearby.

"Yes, Father?"

"Are you about finished? We should be heading home soon."

Yes, she was done. She'd had more than enough for one day. If it hadn't been for William and his brother, she might have decided not to return. At least they appeared genuine. And that made her service more than worthwhile.

If only she didn't have to wait a full week before seeing them again.

"Coming, Father!"

three

"All right." Mrs. Jennings clapped her hands to get everyone's attention. "Let's bring this meeting to order, shall we?"

Annabelle looked around the courtyard. A large number of maple, oak, and elm trees with sparse branches and new buds offered little shade or privacy. Sunlight filtered through the trees and shone bright at the very middle, providing warmth to the otherwise chilly day. She recognized most of the women gathered. Some chose to sit on the whitewashed iron benches at the edges of the cobblestone pathways, while others surrounded the center where Mrs. Jennings stood. Mother and Victoria flanked Annabelle's sides.

"The reason we're gathered here today," Mrs. Jennings continued, "as you all likely know, is to discuss possible ways we can bring additional assistance to those working the potato patches throughout the city."

The self-proclaimed leader of this meeting had been an active member of the nation's first Ladies Aid Society since its inception more than thirty years ago. At that time, she was no older than Annabelle. With her ingenuity and self-sacrificing endeavors, many women looked up to her for leadership and inspiration. She had earned the right to be deemed the honorary matriarch. Annabelle admired her a great deal and was excited to participate today as an active member.

"What about organizing a rotating group of volunteers to make sure the workers receive food at mealtimes?"

This came from Mrs. Olson. Annabelle didn't know her all that well, but her husband was an influential business owner like Father.

Mrs. Jennings gave Mrs. Olson her undivided attention, nodding and showing approval of the suggestion. "Are you speaking of arranging the preparation and distribution of the meals at each of the lots throughout the city?"

"Yes."

"I believe that sounds like a splendid idea." Mrs. Jennings gazed out over all the women gathered. "Do we have a volunteer or two who might be willing to supervise the others involved? You would need to develop a schedule and arrange for the collection of foods prepared as well as oversee the various teams of ladies at each plot."

Mother stepped forward. "I would be both pleased and honored to accept that position."

Annabelle's eyes widened at her mother's offer. It wasn't that she didn't feel Mother could handle the responsibility. On the contrary, she'd never seen another woman so willing to get down in the dirt to help or so able to balance multiple tasks at once with apparent ease. No, she simply thought Mother had more than enough other commitments without adding one more. But perhaps some of that work had diminished in light of the current economic state.

"My daughters, Annabelle and Victoria, will assist me." Mother moved to place a hand on both Annabelle's and Victoria's shoulders.

What? Not only had Mother volunteered to oversee this new idea, but now she was offering Annabelle's services as well? What about the charity work she already performed or the water she had already committed to deliver? She glanced first at Victoria, who merely shrugged with an amused grin, then up at Mother, who glanced down with a soft smile. It was difficult to deny the unspoken request. They would be working together as a family, after all. She only wished Mother had sought her input first. Well, perhaps she could figure out how to deliver the water and distribute the food at the same time.

"Excellent." Mrs. Jennings nodded once to confirm the arrangement and looked directly at Mother. "I trust you will have no trouble securing more than enough ladies to help. But I'll leave you to that."

All right, so that was done. No backing out now. Annabelle simply had to share her concerns about the water delivery with Mother and work that into this new responsibility. Mother had always been supportive of charitable endeavors, no matter how small. They could come up with a compromise here, too.

"Very well," Mrs. Jennings continued. "With the food distribution arranged, does anyone have other ideas for how we can assist those in need?"

"We could go around again collecting old or extra pieces of clothing."

"What about making sure the seed sacks and potato sprouts for planting are available to the workers?"

"With school coming to a close soon, there is a need for care for the younger children who are unable to work."

The suggestions flew among the group like bubbles rising from a boiling pot of water. Annabelle had a difficult time keeping up with everything. Mrs. Jennings seemed to have no trouble, though. In no time at all, at least one woman had been assigned as the head of each project, with promises from others to assist in the area they took the most interest in.

It felt good to know they would be helping in every way possible. Annabelle knew the Ladies Aid could accomplish quite a lot when they put their minds to it, but she'd never seen the progress in action on such a grand scale before today. It was exhilarating. And she could hardly wait to get started.

Mother placed pressure on Annabelle's shoulder, including both of her daughters in her gaze. "So do you have any ideas for how we can organize such a substantial amount of food in a short time?"

"We'll cook it," Victoria offered in her simplistic viewpoint.

Mother's tinkling laugh resembled the chimes they had hanging from the trellis in their backyard. "We will be doing some of the cooking, Victoria, but not all of it."

Annabelle tilted her head to the left and tapped her finger against her lips. "Well, for starters we could determine how many plots there are and which ones will be the center for meal distribution."

"That's putting your mind to work." Mother pressed her lips together and raised her eyebrows in apparent pleasure. "I had a feeling securing your assistance would be a wise decision on my part." A twinkle entered Mother's eyes, and Annabelle returned the smile.

"At first I was surprised you volunteered so quickly. I will help, but I wish we could have talked about it all first."

Mother drew her eyebrows together. "You aren't regretting our involvement, are you? Since you jumped at the opportunity a few weeks ago to get involved, I figured this would be the perfect way for you to accomplish that."

"Oh no." Annabelle rushed to assure Mother. "I don't mind at all. In fact, I am happy to be able to be there among the workers, helping them get the nourishment they need. They work so hard and have so little."

Actually, if she used her previous experience of delivering water as an example, distributing food might not be any easier or produce any better results. But it would mean she'd have yet another excuse to see William and Jacob again. And they were sure to show their appreciation, even if no one else did.

"What is troubling you?" Mother touched her cheek. "I can see something is. You have that crease in your brow above your right eye, and that only appears when you're worried."

"Well. . ." Annabelle paused and looked down at her feet. "You know I've already agreed to deliver water when Father makes his weekly visits to the land he donated."

Mother nodded. "Yes."

"If we get involved with food distribution, will that mean I have to give up that task?"

"I don't see why." Mother shrugged. "We'll likely make the land your father owns our primary station and put other ladies in charge of the other plots of land. That will mean you'll be there quite often at mealtime. You can arrive early or stay later to see to the water dispensing as well."

"I can help deliver water, too." Victoria planted both fists on her hips, her duplicated creased brow evidence of her displeasure with being ignored.

Annabelle flicked one of her sister's curls. "Yes, Victoria, you can help as well. But only on the days when we are all there together."

What Mother detailed would work perfectly. Not only could she visit the plot more often, but she could be there for longer periods of time. Father's trip there didn't last long on her first round. Working with Mother sounded better and better with each passing moment.

Annabelle threw her arms around Mother in a quick hug and stepped back. "Thank you."

"For what, dear?" she asked with a smile.

"I admit, I wasn't too sure about this new venture with the food."

"And now?"

"Now I look forward to it. With so many in need these days and without a lot of activity in the city due to the lack of funds available, we need something to keep us busy."

Mother chucked Annabelle's chin with a forefinger. "Somehow I have a feeling you will not suffer from lack of things to do, my dear." She turned away and looked over her shoulder. "Now I must see to the other ladies who will be working with us. Do feel free to mingle if you wish. Or you can join me over there." She gestured toward a small gathering of women awaiting her instruction.

"I believe I will make my way to the other side of the courtyard. Victoria can come with me. Caroline and Rebecca are there with their mother. I'm sure we can find something to talk about."

"Of that I have no doubt." Mother waved them on their way. "Off with you now. We'll meet back together again in about half an hour over by the south entrance."

"All right."

"Bye, Mother," Victoria called.

Annabelle led her sister around the path and raised a hand to signal their friends. About halfway there, she overheard some murmurs coming from a group of three women standing off to the side. From their pinched faces and curled upper lips, it didn't appear they wanted to be there. They took no notice of Annabelle and Victoria.

"I don't see why so many are eager to get involved helping these families," one woman sneered. "If they lost their investments, they probably weren't wise when making them in the first place."

"Exactly," another agreed. "If you ask me, I think they got what they deserved. They no doubt squandered what they had, and now they're paying the price for their actions."

"How can you say that?" The words were out of Annabelle's mouth before she could stop them.

All three women snapped their heads in her direction. Victoria gasped but otherwise remained silent.

"Excuse me?"

Annabelle stepped closer to the trio. "I asked how you could say such a thing about these families in need. Not all of them come from undesirable backgrounds." She thought of the Berringer family. "Some truly are suffering from uncontrollable circumstances."

The first woman looked Annabelle up and down and raised one eyebrow. "Aren't you Felicity Lawson's daughter?"

"Yes." Annabelle stood tall, proud to be associated with her mother.

"That explains the outburst then," the second woman said.

"I beg your pardon?" What did Mother have to do with her behavior?

"Well, it's no secret, my dear," the first woman began with disdain in her voice, "that your mother has been rather heavily involved in charitable causes for many years now. And that work has taken her into some rather questionable areas of the city. It's no surprise that some of the manners of the people she encounters would rub off on you as well."

The woman's words raised Annabelle's hackles. How dare she insult Mother that way? If she weren't concerned about the repercussions, she might give these ladies a piece of her mind. But that would only give credence to their already misguided allegations. So, instead, she took a calming breath and squared off against the women.

"I don't believe you know my mother well if you feel her manners are anything but impeccable. And I honestly can't understand why you would come to today's meeting if you didn't agree with the purpose. You obviously have no intentions of getting involved." She took a moment to look each woman in the eyes. "However, be that as it may, I'm sorry you feel the need to insult others in order to make your lack of participation justified. As for my sister and me, we will continue on our way and do our best to forget this little altercation even occurred." Annabelle offered the most congenial smile she could muster. "Good day, ladies."

With one hand lifting her skirts and her other at Victoria's back, Annabelle encouraged her sister to again head in the direction where they had started in the first place. They were almost out of earshot—but not quite—when one of the women muttered loud enough for Annabelle to hear, "As I said. Poor manners and an obvious show of disrespect for her elders. That young woman is on her way to following the same footsteps as her mother."

Annabelle smiled. The final remark couldn't have been more accurate, nor provided her with more pleasure. If she became even half the woman her mother was, she'd be pleased. What a shame those women didn't understand the blessings that could come from giving.

☙

"Come on, Berringer. Admit it. You or your little brother here threw dirt at us, and now you're lying about it."

William stood not three feet away from the two men about his age making false accusations against him and Jacob. Their greased-back hair and clothing with holes in it made them look the part of the ruffians they attempted to be. They'd been inventing stories and causing problems for several days now. And William was nearing his tolerance point.

"Yes," the second hoodlum echoed. "We saw you do it."

With a sigh, William glanced down at Jacob to be sure his little brother stood behind him. Then he looked between the two accusers. "That is a bald-faced lie, Charlie, and you know it. Neither Jacob nor I did anything of the sort."

The first man snorted in derision. "Are you saying we made it up?"

"That's exactly what I'm saying, Johnny."

"Then how come the dirt was flung from this direction? There ain't no one around who could've done it except you two."

William clenched his fists and ground his teeth. These two weren't going to go away, but he refused to give in to their taunts. "If dirt truly did fly in your direction, perhaps it was blown by the wind as a result of your digging in it."

"Or you digging and making certain it landed at our feet," Charlie piped in, "instead of keeping it on your own bit of land."

Johnny took a step closer. "You've been swaggering around here for weeks now, acting superior with your fancy talk and making the rest of us feel like scum under your shoes. But you're no better than us, and we're gonna prove it."

Charlie thumped his right fist into his palm. "Right here, right now. Let's see how much of a man you really are."

William fought hard not to roll his eyes at their attempts to intimidate him. Two against one should have made him a little wary, but these two were more filled with hot air than true mettle.

"Come on, Willie," Jacob said from behind. "Show them what you got."

The other two chuckled. "You even got yourself a cheering section."

"Jacob, you stay out of this," William growled. "Father will have both our heads if we get into a fight."

"Oh, so you're still answering to Daddy now, are you?" Johnny taunted. "Why don't you send little Jacob here running on home to tattle on us? Then maybe you won't have to hide behind your kid brother instead of facing us like a man."

The tic in William's jaw started pounding like crazy. His lungs expanded and contracted at a faster pace, despite everything he did to calm himself. These two were asking for trouble, and he'd give it to them if they didn't stop. Then he remembered that Jacob stood right there behind him. If he did send his brother scurrying to Father, he'd never hear the end of it. But if he lowered himself to fight Johnny and Charlie, Jacob might learn the wrong way to deal with men like these two bullies. No, he had to stay in control—for both their sakes.

"So what's it gonna be, Berringer?" Johnny narrowed his eyes then kicked dirt at William. "The way I see it, you got two choices."

"You're right, Johnny, I do." William swallowed, fighting hard to keep back the growl in the back of his throat. "You can say whatever you wish about me. You can even make up lies about things that never happened." He took a step forward and stared directly into Johnny's face, clenching his fists again until he could almost feel his nails puncturing the skin. "But I will not engage in any form of a fight with you. Not now or ever."

A flash of hesitation appeared in Johnny's eyes then disappeared. The man swallowed, not once but twice, before taking an almost imperceptible step back. William tried not to grin at the obvious show of anxiety. He might not agree to fight Johnny, but at least he could leave the man with his dignity still intact—what little there was, anyway.

Several moments of silence passed. Johnny didn't break his gaze, and Charlie stood there waiting to see what would happen. The leader of the two was clear.

Finally, Johnny released a slow breath. "Come on, Charlie. These two just ain't worth our time."

Charlie took a moment for the words to sink in. "You mean we aren't gonna fight today?"

"Not today, no." Johnny leveled a menacing glare at William. "Maybe another time when little boys aren't around to get in the way."

As if Jacob could stop William if things got too out of hand. Sure, he'd do what he could to spare his brother from such violence, but he had his limits, too.

Johnny turned to leave, and Charlie followed, but not before delivering one final parting remark.

"You just watch your back, Berringer. Because when you least expect it, we'll be there."

William had no doubt Charlie spoke the truth. And if that time came, he might not have much of a choice. For now, though, he had managed to avoid the immediate problem. Oh, how he wished he could've taught those two a lesson.

four

"Look at all this food, Annabelle!" Victoria walked up and down the length of the table, eyes wide. If she weren't attempting to maintain her ladylike appearance, she'd likely be licking her lips as well.

"Yes, I only wish it hadn't rained so hard last night." Annabelle lifted her boot again and grimaced at the mud caked on the bottom. The hem of her skirts had become soiled the moment she set foot on the land from the stone-paved sidewalks.

The fare being set out on the solid tables tantalized her taste buds. From bean soup, braised beef, and boiled asparagus, to great mounds of mashed potatoes and cherry pie for dessert, the ladies had worked hard to create a delicious meal sure to have the workers coming in droves.

"So when will we begin serving?" Victoria nearly bounced in excitement. "I love the idea of being a food angel."

Annabelle smiled, her heart warming at her sister's tenderness. It helped having someone else eager to serve working alongside her. Most of the women had willingly prepared the foods and even helped transport them. All but a few of them ceased their efforts or were unwilling to engage when it actually came to interacting with the workers. But that's where Annabelle knew the true joy came. To see the gratitude on their faces and know they were getting a warm meal meant a lot to her.

At least she hoped she'd see their thankfulness. A part of her wondered if the reception would be as cold as last week with the water. No sense fretting about that now, though.

She had work to do.

"Annabelle," Mother called from a few feet away, "make sure you tie an apron over your clothes. I know we aren't wearing anything that can't get soiled, but we should still do our best to remain as clean as possible."

"I will."

Annabelle stepped away to reach for her apron and tied it around her waist. Then she made a final perusal of the tables to make sure everything was in order. With only ten minutes until the noon break, her hands started twitching. She wanted the workers to come in droves for a hot meal, and she wanted to be busy doing something. But there didn't seem to be anything to do.

"Take this, Annabelle," Mother said from behind her as she carried a pot of braised beef.

Annabelle had been so lost in her own anxiousness that she hadn't heard Mother approach.

"Stir the gravy and make sure to spoon it across all the meat."

Finally! Something to do. She glanced over her shoulder to see her mother smiling.

"The time will pass much faster with a task to complete."

She left before Annabelle could reply. How well Mother knew her. No wonder they worked so well together.

"Can I help with something, too?" Victoria wrapped a hand around Mother's arm and followed along beside her.

"Yes, dear." Mother wrapped an arm around Victoria's waist. "You can help me stir the potatoes and set out the tin plates for serving."

Their words faded as they moved farther away. With spoon and serving fork in hand, Annabelle soaked the pieces of beef farther into the gravy. At least the chill of the morning had turned into another warm day. Otherwise they might not have been able to promise a hot meal to the workers.

They'd been spreading the word for several days to make sure everyone knew.

A bell rang and sounded to everyone that the meal was ready. Annabelle shifted from one foot to the other and drummed her fingers on the table in front of her. No one came toward them, although many did stop their work to take a break. She glanced around at those she could see. They were definitely curious, but they didn't make an attempt to investigate. If they waited too long, the food would be cold, and all their hard work would have been for naught.

So Annabelle got an idea. She left her station and headed for the end of the table. Grabbing a tin plate, she put a small portion of each item on it and moved her way toward the end, where she grabbed a fork and knife. The other women watched, and one nodded when she realized Annabelle's plan.

With a deep breath, she stepped away from the table and headed toward the nearest worker. It happened to be a young father with his wife and two sons, who clung to their mother's skirts and hid partially behind her.

"The hot meal is for everyone," Annabelle began. "Please. Take this and bring your family to get plates of their own." She extended the plate toward him, praying he wouldn't allow his pride to turn down the offering.

The man swallowed several times and looked from the plate to Annabelle and down at his wife. Almost a minute passed before the man slowly raised a hand and took the plate from Annabelle.

"Thank you," he choked out.

She released her breath in a soft sigh and gave the family an encouraging smile, winking at the two boys who seemed to be in awe of her. One of them curled his fingers and gave a little wave then ducked behind his mother again.

"Make sure you get your fill, now. There is more than

enough food for everyone. We don't want anyone to leave hungry."

The family followed her to the table and continued on to the far end. That seemed to be the trigger for the other workers. Before long, a line stretching back at least sixty feet had formed. Parents and children all gathered for the midday meal and a break from their work.

For the next forty minutes, the women filled the plates presented by each worker. With each passing person, Annabelle became more and more delighted to be there. Far better than last week, this endeavor seemed to be paying off in a great way.

In the frantic pace to see everyone fed, Annabelle didn't recall William or Jacob coming to get any food. When the line dissipated, she took a moment to brush her hair back from her face and wipe her hands on her apron, now smeared and in dire need of a good scrubbing. Susannah was going to love doing the wash this week.

Annabelle stepped back and surveyed the small groups of families eating together. Some had already finished and were back at work. Others, no doubt, enjoyed their respite from the backbreaking labor. Her gaze took in each and every cluster of people until she finally located the person she sought.

William crossed a particularly muddy piece of land, with Jacob trailing behind him. Both held a plate, but William walked with purpose in his step. Annabelle followed their progress until they stopped in front of a young lad who couldn't be much more than seven or eight. She couldn't hear the verbal exchange, but the boy dipped his chin toward his chest and shook his head at whatever William said to him. A moment later, William handed the boy his plate. The boy hesitated then took the food and nearly inhaled it.

Why hadn't the boy come through the line like everyone else? Surely he had family somewhere who could have brought him. And why had William not filled up two plates if he intended to give one to the boy?

"What are you looking at, Annabelle?" Victoria appeared at her side and stared across the land in an attempt to identify the source of her sister's attention.

"Nothing, really." Annabelle checked the line and saw that only a handful of workers remained. Some latecomer volunteers had just arrived to help with the cleanup afterward. "Victoria, would you mind taking over my station here and serving anyone who's left?"

"I can do that. Where are you going?"

"To help a friend," was all she said to her sister. Victoria didn't need to know any more. It would only start a slew of questions Annabelle wasn't ready to answer just yet.

After filling another plate, she made her way to where William and Jacob had settled, sharing one tin plate between them. They'd located some higher ground and were able to sit on a clear patch of dirt. William looked up and stood when she approached, but he didn't offer a greeting of any kind.

Jacob turned his head when his brother moved and beamed a wide grin at her. "Good afternoon, Miss Annabelle." His face was smeared with gravy, and his fingers bore evidence of the rather large piece of cherry pie he'd sampled.

Annabelle giggled at the adorable sight, retrieving a clean napkin from her skirt pocket for him. "Good afternoon, Jacob. I see you're enjoying your lunch."

"It's the best meal we've had in weeks." He tilted his head and regarded her with a curious stare as he eyed the plate of food she held. "Did you come to eat with us, too?"

William narrowed his eyes. That wasn't exactly a welcome invitation if she *had* intended to join them. Did he just not want her around, or was there some other reason for his seeming distrust?

"No, Jacob. I actually brought your brother an extra plate

since he gave his away."

At this William averted his gaze and looked down at the ground.

"He saw this little boy who didn't have anything to eat, so he took his plate to make sure the boy wouldn't go hungry. His papa didn't want to come and take the free food, and we felt bad. So we gave him some of ours."

"Well, that was very kind and generous of you, Jacob." She raised her eyes toward William, who had returned his gaze to her. "Of both of you." Focusing again on the plate she held, she continued. "Will you accept this plate from me, then?"

He took the plate and split portions of it with Jacob before partaking on his own.

"Why did you go to all the trouble to bring this to me?"

So he was still sore about something. And he couldn't accept a gift for what it was. He had to question it. Annabelle had no idea why, but she figured the honest answer would be the best way to go.

"Because the Lord commands us to help those in need and watch out for the ones among us who have fallen on bad times."

"That's what the Bible says," Jacob announced, pride evident in his voice.

"You're exactly right, Jacob. The Bible does teach us that." So they had some exposure to the teachings in the scriptures. That was a start. "It also commands us to love our neighbors and even do good to those who hurt us."

"Mama used to read to us all the time before we had to come here to work. Now we don't get to hear the stories as often because she's so tired at night that she falls asleep right away."

"Well, she works hard, Jacob," William interjected. "You can't expect her to do all the things she used to do when we had our house and lived a different life." He grunted.

"Besides, a lot of what she read was just stories of people who lived a long time ago. We've got more important things to do these days."

More important things than reading the Bible and learning from what God has to say? Annabelle couldn't imagine anything that could take the place of God in her life.

"Do you mind if I join you? I've been standing for quite some time and would love to take a rest."

"Sure!" Jacob scooted over and made a grand show of brushing a clear spot in the dirt beside him.

Annabelle hesitated and looked to William before making a move. He didn't say a word, only nodded. She gathered her skirts in her hands and settled next to Jacob. William took a seat as well and continued eating.

"Jacob, you say that your mother used to read a lot to you. What was your favorite story?"

"Umm. . ." He scrunched up his face and pressed his lips together, thinking hard. "Well, I like the story of Jacob, but that's only because we have the same name." He grinned. "The other one I like is the one about the boy who only had two fish and five loaves of bread, but the men who followed Jesus fed thousands of men with it."

"Yes, that's an amazing story, isn't it?"

"You fed a lot of people today with the food you brought, and it was much better than fish and bread."

"They fed a lot of people," William interjected, "because they all made a lot of food and brought it. God had nothing to do with it."

"Actually, William, God has everything to do with it."

William waved her off and remained intent on the food still left on his plate.

"We wouldn't be here if God didn't command us to be. And we wouldn't spend any time at all with those in need if we weren't following His commandments."

"So you're saying you don't really want to be here. That you're only doing it because you feel you have to or because of some obligation?"

All right, so that didn't go exactly as she'd planned. She wanted him to see that she cared, as did all the other women, and that's why they came. But he was being rather hard-headed about it.

"No," she corrected. "We *do* want to be here. At least I do. My mother and sister do as well. The three of us are organizing the food distribution. We enjoy helping those who are working hard here at the potato patches and farm plots. It's an added bonus when we can get involved in others' lives instead of just sitting at home and collecting items for people we'll never see."

"Well, don't feel you need to spend any more time than necessary with us. We're doing just fine on our own and don't need your charity."

Annabelle almost recoiled from the bitter tone in his voice. His words stung. On the one hand, he appeared to appreciate her efforts. On the other, his words and attitude said something entirely different.

"I don't consider it charity at all, Mr. Berringer. In fact, I see it as a partnership in many ways."

William wrinkled his brow. "How so?"

"Well, you and many other families are spending your days working this land and cultivating it for fresh food that will be harvested and used to feed those in the city who need it. Some of what you harvest will replenish the depleted stores that are in desperate need of restocking." She gestured back over her shoulder toward where the women were cleaning up the food. "It's our pleasure to provide a hot meal for you as our way of saying thank you." Annabelle shrugged. "A partnership."

He regarded her for several moments, as if he couldn't

believe someone like her would bother to spend time with someone like him. But she'd seen passion in him that obviously ran quite deep. And despite the heartaches of recent months, she knew that spark still existed. She also longed to know more about his life before they lost everything. And she'd only find that out if she spent time with him. If he didn't welcome her presence, she could always come to visit Jacob instead. Jacob watched his brother with interest but remained silent. She prayed William's sour attitude didn't rub off on Jacob. That innocence suited the boy well and didn't deserve to be tainted.

"You make some valid points, but I still don't agree that God is involved in any way."

"What makes you say that?"

"If He were making it possible for you to be here, then why didn't He make it possible for the banks to survive the crisis or the railroads not to lose their investments? Why did He cause so many families to lose their homes and their entire livelihoods?" William balanced the plate on his legs and flailed both arms out away from his body. "God caused the selective ruin of many families who didn't deserve to suffer the way they have. He picked and chose at will, while others came out of this just fine. If He is so intent on helping, why didn't He help then?"

Annabelle remained silent for several moments. He asked a lot of good questions. Questions she didn't know if she could answer. After all, she was among the families who faired far better than his had. What could she say to him that would ease the obvious anger and resentment he felt?

"You make some valid arguments, and I know I don't have all the answers—"

"Look," he cut her off. "I appreciate all that you're trying to do. The food was delicious, and you managed to feed a lot of people. But no matter what you do, you can't cure everything.

And regardless of what you might find to say, it's not going to change our circumstances any." He gathered Jacob's plate and stacked it on top of his own then handed them to her.

She took them and stood there, waiting for what he might say next. The pain he felt was evident, yet she could see he kept his emotions somewhat in check and made certain to deliver a respectful response to her. No retort came to mind to what he'd said already, yet he seemed to need to get a few things off his chest. So she lingered.

"The truth is, God decided we must have needed some sort of reprimand or punishment. Maybe we weren't doing good enough to please Him. Whatever the reason, we lost what we had, and your family didn't." He schooled his expression and reached out to take Jacob's arm. "So thank you for coming and bringing the extra plate. But we can't stand around and talk all day. There is work that needs to be done." Bending to retrieve his cap, he straightened and slapped it on his head. "Good day, Miss Lawson."

five

"Now wait just a moment."

William didn't pause at Annabelle's retort, but he grimaced at the predictable response. He knew she wouldn't just leave his good-bye at that. She didn't seem the type. He fought against a grin that threatened to pull at his lips at the appealing prospect of continuing conversation with her. Despite her pleasing appearance, he didn't look forward to more talk of God.

"William," Jacob said in a loud whisper. "Aren't we going to wait for Miss Annabelle?"

"She'll be able to keep pace with us, Jacob. We're not walking all that fast."

"But why did we walk away? I don't think she was done talking."

"Mr. Berringer, I don't believe we were finished with our conversation." She spoke as if she'd heard Jacob.

William wanted to say that a woman like Annabelle could probably find any number of reasons to talk, but that wouldn't be fair to her. He'd only had two encounters with her, after all. Too soon to be making assumptions like that.

"We left because our break is over, and we have to get back to work. I know you might want to stay and talk with Miss Annabelle, but our ground isn't going to till itself. And if we want to make sure we have something to show for the first harvest, we have to put our backs into it."

He turned his head to look down at Jacob, but in his peripheral vision, he caught sight of Annabelle still trailing behind them, stepping gingerly through the mud patches.

46

She'd somehow dispensed with the tin plates he'd handed her, so perhaps another volunteer came to take them. He and Jacob just tromped along, mud and all. If his mother saw him right now, she'd box his ears for leaving a young woman the way he had.

A groan rumbled in his throat.

"What's the matter, Willie?"

"Nothing. We should stop, though, and wait for Miss Annabelle. It's not nice to leave her trudging through the mud on her own."

Jacob immediately halted in his tracks and turned, beaming a wide smile in Annabelle's direction. "We'll wait for you, Miss Annabelle. Come on. The mud isn't that bad."

William grinned. Leave it to Jacob to make an unpleasant experience sound like fun. He paused as well but didn't turn around as he allowed his brother to draw Annabelle into their circle. His brother even reached out a hand to help her attain the last step that brought her to their sides. How could an eight-year-old boy make him feel like such a lout?

"Thank you very much, Jacob."

She raised the hem of her skirts just enough to view her boots, stamped each one of them twice to shake off the caked mud, and then lowered her skirts again. Giving her blouse a somewhat discreet tug, she appeared to have herself back in order. At least they were on dry ground now for the remainder of their trek.

"Shall we continue?" William extended his left arm out, palm up in front of them.

It was more of an instruction than a question, and he resumed walking without waiting for a response.

"I would like to pick up our conversation where we left off, Mr. Berringer." Annabelle sounded a little winded, but she kept up with them.

"And I would like to get back to work, Miss Lawson." He

almost cringed at the harsh tone to his voice. It was true, though. "Fields don't plant themselves, you know," he added, repeating what he'd said to Jacob only moments before.

"I realize that, Mr. Berringer. And be that as it may, there still remains the issue of your beliefs regarding the role God played in the ruination of your family and so many others."

She didn't give up easily, did she? He'd have to add persistence to the list of qualities he'd begun making in his mind. Only he didn't know if that one went under positive or negative attributes.

"Willie, do you really think God caused us to lose our money?"

Jacob spoke with such curiosity, yet a tinge of worry accompanied his question as well. William scolded himself for allowing his younger brother to overhear the exchange. It was bad enough he struggled with understanding the situation. Jacob didn't need to be dragged into the quandary as well.

William paused and crouched next to his brother, placing a hand on his shoulder and looking up slightly to meet his brother's eyes. "Hey, Jacob, why don't you run on over and see if Father has a new job for you to do? I bet you're tired of digging holes in the ground. Maybe they have the extra seeds for the parts we've already dug."

"Really?" Jacob's eyes brightened, and he seemed to forget the question he'd just asked. "Do you think he'll let me plant instead of dig?"

"Won't know unless you go ask and find out, now will you?" William grinned in hopes of enticing his brother even more.

"Yes!" Jacob threw his arms around William's neck. "Thanks, Willie."

And off he went, racing across the expanse of land and carefully avoiding the rows that were already done.

Annabelle watched alongside him. A moment later she spoke. "That was sweet of you to do that for Jacob."

William shrugged. "He's been clamoring to switch up his tasks for several days now."

She kept her gaze on Jacob and tilted her head to the right, pressing her lips into a thin line. "There is such a difference in your ages, yet you treat him like any older brother would."

He closed his eyes and sighed. "Mother and Father actually lost two others between Jacob and me." Yet another reason to be angry at God.

Annabelle released a soft gasp. "Oh, Mr. Berringer, I'm so sorry."

William opened his eyes to see the stricken look on her face. A part of him wanted to respond to her compassion, but the other part didn't want to get into anything else. The latter won.

"It was a long time ago," he said with a shrug. "But we are a bit protective of him." Then there was the obvious reason. "And he didn't need to be here listening to this conversation."

"Does that mean you're willing to continue our discussion?"

He paused and looked at the sky. The sun blazed overhead, unimpeded by clouds or shade of any kind. After the recent rains and chill in the air, the warmth brought a welcome change. He then turned his attention to the seemingly endless stretch of land they had been given to farm. Finally, he shifted his attention to Annabelle.

"Miss Lawson, I will be honest with you. This topic of God's involvement is one I'm sure you would love to discuss at great lengths. But as I told Jacob and as I mentioned a moment ago, there is a lot of work to be done. I just can't stand around all day talking."

"Then show me what needs to be done, and I'll help."

William started to open his mouth then snapped it shut.

Had she really just offered to work alongside him? And if so, why? It couldn't only be so she could share her point of view and hope to change his mind. Because if that was the case, she was wasting her time. And what about her mother and father? Surely they wouldn't approve of her working alone with him out here without supervision.

"I, uh. . .I don't know that there's anything you can do." Her simplistic solution to the closed door he'd attempted to present on the discussion unsettled him. And he didn't want to invite unnecessary trouble from her parents should they learn of her whereabouts.

Annabelle looked around. "There are a lot of women working in these fields. I'm not exactly as delicate as I might appear. Besides, with me working as well, you will have no excuse left to avoid conversation."

Or so she thought. He could remain silent and refuse to answer her questions if he so chose. Something told him, though, that she wouldn't be deterred so easily. It seemed he had no choice but to go along with her.

"All right." He pointed to an untilled section of land to their left. "I began working there this morning. Let me fetch some additional tools and seed, and we can work those rows."

"Very well." She didn't waste a moment before heading in that direction where he'd pointed.

William marched off to do as he said. If she was that determined to work alongside him, so be it. Perhaps he could get so involved in the tilling that he wouldn't be required to say much in response to what he was sure would only amount to preaching.

Five minutes later, he met her at their work plot and dumped a heavy bag of seed at her feet. After that came a bucket of water. The liquid sloshed over the sides when he dropped it on the ground. His hoe and digging stick remained nestled in the hollow of his shoulder.

"You'll be using the seeds to fill the holes I dig. Then you'll need to pour a good measure of water over them to moisten the soil."

"I believe I can handle that."

William thought he detected a hint of sarcasm in her voice, but he didn't bother to look at her to find out if his suspicions were correct.

"All right, then. Let's get started."

He dug the hoe into the earth and broke apart the clumps of dirt. With the digging stick, he pressed down the dirt and made a suitable hole, then stood back and waited for Annabelle to fill it. She did as he'd instructed, refilling the hole and pouring water over it.

"Good. Let's continue."

It was the closest he could come to a compliment. Best not to encourage her too much. She learned fast, though—with just the right number of seeds and an appropriate amount of water. She worked as if she had done this before. But that was ridiculous. From what he could tell, they'd both grown up in similar households. She was a lady. Servants most likely performed the menial tasks of planting and gardening. Still, she didn't seem to mind the labor.

He moved on to the next hole and then the next. After digging and filling at least a dozen, he tilted his head and regarded her from the corner of his eye. She reached into the seed sack and withdrew two handfuls. Curious, he paused as she deposited the seeds into a front pocket of her apron, which still bore evidence of the meal she'd helped serve for lunch.

William cleared his throat. "Impressive," was all he could manage. He still hadn't come to terms with her offer to help. And now she seemed to be making the best of things.

"If we are to be as productive as possible, this will help our pace. The sack can be left at the end of each row, and I can replenish as needed." She smiled, obviously pleased with her ingenious solution.

"Good thinking," he said cautiously, determined not to tip the tone of this forced situation one way or the other. He moved ahead to dig the next hole. "The work is not done with digging and planting, though. The seeds must be tended and nurtured each day. Then the weeds will need to be cleared away to allow room for the seeds to take root and sprout. After that, there's the elimination of any pests that might take up residence on the leaves or the plants." He looked down at the ground and spoke low. "There will be much to do long after you're gone."

Annabelle dug into her pocket for more seeds, but not before William caught the flash of disappointment in her eyes at his intentional barb. She waited in pronounced silence until he had the next hole ready, then dumped in the seeds, filled the hole, and poured the water.

It was just as well. The less communication they had, the easier it would be to get lost in his work. But the longer the silence lasted, the more his conscience was pricked by guilt. If she said something, he might be tempted to deliver an insult in order to protect himself. That went against his grain. He might not be sure where he stood as far as God was concerned, but he was still a gentleman. And as such, he had a duty to be courteous and respectful.

If only she didn't make it so difficult.

As she filled the most recent hole, she paused and stared at the wet area left behind by the water. "These seeds are a lot like us," she muttered almost to herself.

He drew his eyebrows together as she turned her head to look up at him.

"These seeds. They are a lot like people." She reached into her apron and pulled out a few, holding them in her palm. "In their present state, they are like a newborn baby. After we are born, we need a great deal of care and attention in order to grow in the best environment possible. Our roots are formed from the instruction of our mother and father and other people in our lives."

He moved down the row, working as she spoke. A stolen glance at his companion's face revealed bright eyes and an eagerness in her expression. She obviously assumed that he was interested in what she had to say. He may be, but he didn't intend to tell her that.

"When we are ready," she continued, "we break free from our family—like what you will do when the vegetables are ready for picking—and we become mature plants. We are independent, but we came from the same roots. If conditions are right, the seeds at the core of the vegetable are strong enough to be replanted in the ground in the hopes that they will grow to produce healthy plants. Just like their sources before them. And so the cycle continues, does it not?"

William rammed the hoe into the ground and separated the dirt. "I never thought of farming and family in that way."

"Our faith in God is almost the same."

He gripped the long end of the hoe, making a fist around the rough wood. *God again*, he groaned inwardly. Why did she insist upon making such an analogy to his faith? It would have been fine to leave it as a parallel to their physical growth. He didn't want to hear anything about God or how the roots his parents had instilled in him still ran deep.

Besides, his life couldn't possibly be compared to these seeds or the way they would be tended as they grew. God had uprooted him and his family from the comfort of their home and left them to wither and die without sustenance. It was by pure chance they had happened upon this opportunity to farm in order to have a way of life again.

"We begin as little seeds when we first believe. By reading the Bible and going to church with others who believe, we receive the nourishment and the care to grow healthy and strong."

William tried to ignore Annabelle's words, but no other noise existed to drown them out. It was impossible not to hear them.

"We live each day to the fullest and plant seeds in others to help them grow as we grow. If our faith is strong, when the rain and winds and storms come, we will survive."

The winds and storms hadn't stopped since the runs on the banks had ripped the rug out from under his family and forced them to lose their home. Sure, they were surviving, but not by God's help. He'd had to compromise his own goals, dreams, and desires. He'd been forced to use his own innovation to make the best of the situation. He was working hard, just as his parents and his brother were, all so they could start rebuilding what they had lost. No matter what Annabelle said or how much time she took to extend her charity to others, she wouldn't change the facts.

Although, if he had to admit it, he was enjoying her company far more than he thought he would—more than he should, all things considered. As they moved up and down the rows, his mind focused on Annabelle. She didn't have to be here working with him. And she didn't have to get mud and sweat and dirt all over her pretty clothes. Yet she was here doing exactly that. And for what? For him? That possibility seemed too far-fetched to even consider. What if it was true, though? He couldn't do anything about it. He had nothing to offer a fine lady like her. Not now, anyway.

"Is everything all right, Mr. Berringer?"

Her voice interrupted his musings.

"Your face is rather flushed. I do hope you aren't suffering from heatstroke or even from the food we prepared for your lunch."

William shook himself free from his trailing thoughts. He

risked a look in her direction. Loose tendrils of her chestnut hair framed her face, and the slightest bit of perspiration formed on her brow. Despite the soiled state of her clothing, she presented a rather appealing picture. For a fleeting moment, he entertained thoughts of the many possibilities. But the worried expression gracing her delicate features reminded him of the folly of those thoughts and brought him back to the present.

"No, no," he rushed to assure her. "There was nothing wrong with the food, and I am feeling just fine. I promise."

William took note of the progress they'd made. If they continued at this pace, they'd complete at least five rows before the hour was done. Had it not been for her creative use of the pocket in her apron, they no doubt would have been slowed considerably. If only she didn't feel the need to ramble on and on about faith and God and strong roots.

"In that case," she replied, "I had another thought regarding your comments earlier."

And there she was, back on the religious talk again. Rather than respond, he remained quiet and focused on the planting. *Let her continue to talk to herself. Perhaps that audience will be preferable to my participation in the conversation.*

She continued as if she didn't even notice his silence. "You seem to believe that God has forgotten all about you. Or that He's too busy to notice that your family is in need and suffering like so many others."

Annabelle followed behind him, focused on her part of the work and what she felt the need to say to him.

"But God doesn't forget the tiniest sparrow, and He hasn't forgotten you or your family, Mr. Berringer. Why else would you have this land to farm and the help of others in this city to assist you in rebuilding? Why else would your entire family have been left healthy and able to work to recover from the loss?"

His mind drifted back nearly twenty years to his child-hood and a time when he sat on his mother's lap listening to her read from the Bible. He remembered the story of the sparrow, as well as the lilies in the field. His mother had told him that God valued him far above those items and that he should never worry about tomorrow. God had it all under control.

"You realize, Mr. Berringer, that you could have been more than crippled in your finances. Illness, injury, or any number of other setbacks could have incapacitated you or one of your family members. And then where would you be?"

William wanted so desperately to say something to her. But words failed him. What would he say, though? He couldn't exactly throw off everything when deep down in his heart he knew she spoke the truth. Still, there was a rather large gap between what he'd learned as a child and what he lived today as an adult.

Annabelle didn't press him in any way. And soon, assum-ing either his disinterest or his inner struggle, she lapsed into silence as well. The silence chilled him like the cold April rains that had recently fallen. At least they agreed on some-thing. Not talking would prevent any disagreements or argu-ments. And since their conversations to this point seemed to end in some form of conflict, maybe silence was the answer.

"Annabelle!"

They both looked up at the calling of her name. It took William a moment to locate the source. A young girl, who looked to be four or five years older than his brother, stood about seventy-five feet away, shielding her eyes from the overhead sun and looking in their direction.

"That's my younger sister, Victoria," Annabelle explained. "She's no doubt coming to say it's time to go home."

William looked back over their progress. They had reached the end of the sixth row. More than he had expected they'd do in the time they'd been working.

Annabelle made a point to carry the nearly empty water pail to the start of the next row. William followed her as she walked toward where they'd left the seeds. She reached into her apron and emptied the seeds back into the sack. Then she dusted off her hands and stood staring at the ground.

He couldn't tell if she was trying to think of something to say or waiting for him to say something. Again, his conscience pricked. He couldn't let her leave without at least thanking her for her help.

"Uh, Miss Lawson? I, uh. . ." Why wouldn't his brain work? This should be a simple task. He cleared his throat and waited for her to look at him. "Thank you. For your help and for what you shared today about faith and God."

Oh no. Where had that come from? He had only intended to mention the work. Yet for all he tried, he couldn't stop the tumbling words from his mouth. "I know I didn't say much, but I did hear every word you said. You've given me a lot to think about."

Hope filled her eyes, making the dark blue hue lighten a few shades. "Mr. Berringer, if I only succeeded in making you rethink where you stand with God, then that's enough for me. I don't wish to preach, but I believe in my heart that God will never leave or forsake us. I would love for you to see that, too."

Her innocence struck a chord with him, and her open expression compelled him in ways he didn't understand.

"I can't promise anything except that I will continue to think on it."

She nodded. "And that's more than enough." With a glance over her shoulder and a raised arm, she signaled her sister then returned her gaze to him. "Thank you for allowing me to work beside you today, Mr. Berringer. And I hope we see each other again." She grasped her skirt in her hand

and smiled. "Good day."

"Good day, Miss Lawson," he said as she walked away toward her sister.

At least that parting hadn't been as cruel as the one he'd delivered right after lunch. This one left them with a chance to at least remain cordial. Although, after all that she'd said to him and the time she'd spent working at his side, they were now beyond mere polite exteriors. Where they stood, he couldn't say. But he admired her tenacity and hoped their paths would cross again soon.

six

Annabelle accepted the assistance of the footman as she descended from the carriage onto the sidewalk. Victoria, Matthew, and her parents followed. The five of them approached the impressive home of Mayor Pingree on Woodward. It was quite a few blocks from their home on Marietta, but the ride had passed quickly.

Now, standing in front of the house for the first time, Annabelle studied the Italianate-style architecture with French influence. She'd heard about the mayor's taste for things French and read a great deal about the French influence in some of the major cities throughout America. However, she had no idea he'd go to lengths such as this to bring a taste of France to Detroit. Even the mansard roof seemed out of place among the other structures.

"Isn't it beautiful, Annabelle?" Victoria came to stand next to her sister, transfixed and staring at the home in front of them.

"Yes, Victoria. It's stunning."

A handful of elm trees grew tall and protected the home, set back about forty feet from the street. Two brick walks wound away from Woodward, one to the mayor's home and the other to the carriage house that sat farther back. It was the middle of May, and the wide variety of flowers planted at the front of the home blossomed in an array of colors, shapes, and sizes.

"Come now, girls," Mother reprimanded softly. "Let's not dawdle and appear impolite. I am certain many of the guests have already arrived, and we don't wish to be tardy."

The five of them walked up the five stone steps to the

front porch where a butler swung wide the door and ushered them inside. After taking their wraps, he directed them into the parlor to the right. A maid weaved her way through the other guests and held a tray of glasses filled with punch, wine, and champagne.

Annabelle took a glass of punch and sipped it as she stepped away from her parents to observe the furnishings of the room. The deeply tufted sofas and chairs were covered in crimson and black satin damask. The rosewood frames, delicately carved, had recently been polished until the wood gleamed. A grand piano sat in the corner, where a young gentleman tinkled out soft strains of a pleasing melody. Even the satin drapes that hung from the doorway at the far end matched the crimson of the carpet under her feet. And the oval end tables were graced with sienna marble instead of the white slab marble they had at home.

The various items placed here resembled their parlor, but the quality far outshone anything they had. Annabelle could only imagine the expense involved if the entire home had been decorated in the same manner. The quality alone likely cost the mayor twice as much as what her parents had paid to decorate their home. The only aspects that seemed to parallel her home were the wallpaper patterns and the chandelier that hung from the ceiling in the center of the room.

Annabelle felt almost like an imposter. It seemed wrong somehow to be standing in a room this ornate when families such as William's shared the open space of an abandoned warehouse near their farm plot with at least four or five other families. She'd been serving the families on the land her father had donated for more than a month now, and she'd even begun to view her own home in a different light.

Victoria sidled up to her. "Feels strange, doesn't it? Seeing all the expensive things here," her sister said as if she'd read Annabelle's thoughts.

"Yes, it does. The mayor must have spent a small fortune to decorate his home. I don't suppose we can fault him much, though. This house was built twenty years ago and paid for with money he'd accumulated through his business ventures prior to becoming a mayor. He's done a lot of good for the city and those in need since the financial panic last year."

"He has, I agree." Victoria nodded. "And a man as important as Mayor Pingree shouldn't have to live in anything less simply because others are struggling."

"Still, I can't help but think of the people who are working on Father's land."

"You mean families like the Berringers?"

Annabelle looked down at her sister to see a gleam in the young girl's eyes and a grin on her lips. "Why do you mention them?"

"Father has a list of all the families who are working on that acreage. When I came to find you a couple weeks ago, I asked a few questions and found my answers."

Quite the little detective. Annabelle was impressed. "Well, yes. That family is one in particular. But there are many others working there as well."

"What's so special about the Berringer family, then? You seem to spend a lot of time with them each week or mention them more often than others."

Annabelle shrugged. "I met the two sons the first day I delivered water to the workers, and they were among the only ones to show any true form of gratitude. I guess they stick out in my mind." No reason to make any more of William than necessary. Otherwise her sister would never let it rest.

"Oh. Okay."

She looked about to say something else, but they were interrupted by the arrival of the butler.

"Dinner is served, ladies and gentlemen. Please make your way to the dining room."

Annabelle and Victoria joined the flow of guests as they moved from the parlor and headed toward the dining room. If the first room had been impressive, this one was extraordinary. Several large mirrors with gilded frames flanked two of the three walls. A large portrait of Mayor Pingree adorned the wall behind the head of the table, and three stately windows with brocade curtains were spaced a few feet apart on the fourth wall.

The polished mahogany table in the center of the room gleamed, and when Annabelle found her seat, she could see her reflection in the surface. She smiled at seeing she had been seated next to Mrs. Jennings with Mother on her right. Across the table, Matthew faced her with Victoria and Father flanking his sides. Oh, if only William could be here. Then again, how would that be possible? She knew his family had lost a great deal, but she didn't know for sure just where they stood financially before the crisis. He might not have been included in the guest list for this evening. And being here, or even hearing about it, would only increase his bitterness about his present circumstances.

Her thoughts were once again interrupted by the arrival of their host. Mayor Pingree stood behind his seat at the head of the table and rested his hands on the high back.

"I'd like to thank everyone for coming this evening. From all reports, many of you have been involved in helping launch the efforts to establish the potato patches throughout the city. Others have provided additional clothing, food, and funds, which have gone far toward replenishing our depleted stores." He looked down the table, his gaze resting on each guest on both sides of the table. "I couldn't think of a better way to thank you than to invite you and your families here to enjoy a delicious meal."

After pulling out his chair and taking a seat, he extended his arms out toward his guests.

"Please. Sit. Let's get this dinner under way."

Several servants assisted the ladies present then reached for the napkins on the table, fanning them out before placing them in the ladies' laps.

In a matter of moments, the soft din of voices rose from the table. Mrs. Jennings leaned close.

"My dear, I am quite pleased at the company in which I find myself. I cannot imagine a more giving or industrious family than your own." The woman smiled past her at Annabelle's mother. "Felicity, you have set a fine example for both of your daughters, and it's wonderful to see them following in your footsteps."

Father winked across the table, while Mother nodded at Mrs. Jennings. "Thank you, Olivia," Mother said, pride reflected on her face. "I am quite honored to have two such dutiful daughters and ones so willing to help wherever there is a need."

Salads were placed in front of them, and they halted their conversation for a few moments. After waiting for everyone to be served, they looked to Mayor Pingree to take his first bite. He did and waved his fork in the air to encourage everyone else to do the same.

After eating her first forkful, Mrs. Jennings picked up where they'd left off. "I do know for a fact that the food schedule you have set up, Felicity, is a big success. I haven't seen a more organized distribution since I began working with the Ladies Aid."

"Well, I can't take all the credit," Mother said. "I have a reliable group of ladies who bear the brunt of the work. My daughters and I only work the one plot owned by Brandt. The other areas are under the supervision of many more volunteers."

"Regardless, your work is greatly appreciated."

Father took that moment to speak up as well. "I have heard

various positive discussions from the workers who remained at the factories that were able to stay open regarding the charitable contributions of those who managed to avoid serious declines in their holdings."

"Yes," Mr. Jennings said from Victoria's right. "I'm fortunate the railroad car shop where I serve as supervising manager is still managing to function. After most of the other railroad shops closed along with the stove factories, fear raced through the remaining shops until workers speculated whether or not their job would be next."

"Yet through it all," Mrs. Jennings began, "we as a whole have managed to survive. And I believe a great deal of thanks is owed to our mayor for his innovative ideas."

"I agree," Father echoed. "When the hoped-for revival of business failed to come earlier this spring and the city's poor funds were exhausted, he knew something different was needed."

Matthew leaned forward, his face reflecting interest. "I heard the mayor had analyzed the real estate market from the previous boom in our economy. When he saw all those plots of land being held for a rise in value standing idle all over the city, he made a public appeal to the owners."

Mr. Jennings nodded. "Yes. The mayor asked for permission to use their properties for vegetable gardens, both big and small."

Annabelle had been following the entire story in the newspapers each week ever since the day at church when the pastor had put out a call for donations. Although she didn't often engage in the detailed discussions surrounding the idea, she had found the affectionate name given to the plots rather humorous.

"Pingree's potato patches is what they're being called," she said with a smile. "It does have a nice ring to it, doesn't it?"

Mrs. Jennings chuckled. "It does at that, Annabelle dear.

Several other cities have even taken the model and created similar farming or gardening systems to help their own residents. But it's our very own mayor who is now known as a champion for the needy. It makes me quite proud to be living here in Detroit."

Their salads were removed and replaced by steaming bowls of French onion soup. Considering the home where they were eating, the choice of flavor came as no surprise to Annabelle. She eagerly dug into the delicious broth.

Silence fell upon the table as many took their initial spoonfuls of the second course. A few minutes later, Father resumed the conversation.

"And let's not forget the mayor's fight for municipal ownership of our city's street transportation system."

Mr. Jennings had made quick order of his soup and laid his spoon in the empty bowl, then rested his forearms on the edge of the table. "Yes, he's built more than fifty miles of new track to help our streetcar system."

Victoria sat up straighter in her chair and grinned. "I like that I can ride one for three cents now instead of five like it used to be."

Her childlike fascination with the modernized method of transportation was infectious. Annabelle had ridden on the conveyances on more than one occasion, but Victoria took every opportunity. And since the electric cars had recently replaced the previous horse-drawn ones, Annabelle had to admit enjoying the ride even more.

"Well, if things don't improve with the American Railway Union," Mr. Jennings announced, his face pinched and full of concern, "we might be back to horse-drawn transportation when departing from the confines of a city."

"What do you mean?" Mother asked.

Mr. Jennings's eyes widened. "Have you not heard of the Pullman strike taking place right now? It just started a week ago, so news is only just starting to reach everyone."

"Ah yes." Father nodded. "I read an article about that just this morning in the *Detroit News*."

The next part of their dinner was a refreshing serving of lime sorbet to cleanse their palates in preparation for the main course. Conversation stalled for just a moment as each of them took a small spoonful of the sweet treat.

"Pray tell; do not keep us waiting in suspense much longer, dear," Mother pleaded as soon as her mouth was clear.

"Well, it seems the lack of demand for train cars and the drop in their revenue caused the Pullman Palace Car Company to cut wages by twenty-five percent recently."

"Cut wages?" Matthew's face reflected the horror his voice conveyed. "That's not going to help anyone!"

"I agree," Mr. Jennings stated. "And it seems the workers do as well. Because of their rebellion, this recent strike has brought all transportation west of Chicago to a screeching halt."

Chicago. Annabelle recalled something she'd read awhile back regarding the railway car company. Ah yes, it was the small town that was built. "Isn't Mr. Pullman the man who built a company town near Chicago and paid high wages to the workers who agreed to live there?"

Father looked across the table at her with surprise and pride in his eyes. "I'm impressed, Annabelle, that you're aware of that. And yes, Mr. Pullman is that very same man. The town features attractive houses, complete with indoor plumbing, gas, and sewer systems, plus free education through the eighth grade and a public library."

"Yes," Mother interjected, "but with all that is the reality that Mr. Pullman is controlling everything in that town. He prohibits such things as independent newspapers, public speeches, town meetings, or any speeches that haven't been preapproved by him or his inspectors first."

"Doesn't sound like a desirable place to live," Mrs. Jennings remarked.

Annabelle could think of at least a dozen places that would be more appealing. "It's no wonder the workers have chosen to strike."

"And the strike is gaining popularity rather rapidly." Father sighed. "If something isn't done, it could spread all across the nation. With refusal to load Pullman cars or run trains containing those cars, we could see far-reaching effects even here in Detroit. I pray that doesn't happen."

Silence again fell upon their little group. Annabelle contemplated what some of those effects might be, as if the economic state wasn't enough. It seemed some of the larger companies were bent on making things worse for those already suffering. Didn't they realize the workers were the reason their companies even existed in the first place?

Without workers, they'd have to close their doors permanently. If the owners had been wiser about their investments, they might not have to resort to cutting wages. No guarantees of that existed, but if even a few jobs could be saved, it would be worth it.

From that point forward, talk continued to focus on the improvements being made right there in Detroit and the efforts of so many to rebound from everything. Before Annabelle knew it, the evening had come to a close and they were again in a carriage taking them home.

Father rested his head against the back wall of the carriage and rested his hands over his abdomen. "Well, I must say I enjoyed the evening immensely."

"I never knew Mr. and Mrs. Jennings were so well-informed about current events."

"They'd have to be, Annabelle," Mother answered, "if Mrs. Jennings wants to stay abreast of the current needs in the city to inform the Ladies Aid, and Mr. Jennings wants to make certain his factory remains in operation."

"True." Annabelle could understand that reasoning. And it made for entertaining discussion, even if some moments didn't pique her interest as much as others. It was during those times that her mind drifted to William.

"Father, do you know how many affluent families were affected by the financial crisis?"

He took a deep breath and looked up toward the roof of the carriage. "Well, let's see. Some I know had all their investments tied up in one area. Take the railroad, for instance. When that failed, they lost everything. Others had their money invested in more than one company. But if the majority of those closed due to the railroad failures or the bank runs, they also would have lost a substantial amount."

Annabelle nodded. "And then there is us. We suffered, but not as heavily as some, right?"

"Exactly. Thanks to the investments made by my father and Grandfather Chambers, our surplus was spread out in a diverse number of companies. Some of them faired rather well when the panic struck. Others didn't. But because we had spread out our investments, we weren't hit as hard."

She wondered if William's family had been one of the ones to have everything tied up in one company or in several that came to ruin. Either way, he and his family were forced to work the land her father had donated while she and her family remained in their comfortable home. They had seen the need to cut back on certain frivolous spending, but they were in no danger of losing anything that might cause a drastic change in their lifestyle.

For once she wondered how much truth there was to William's feelings on the matter. Just how had God decided which families would suffer and which wouldn't? The misfortune did seem to strike at random. What made their family worthy of being spared?

Of course, that started another line of thought—the purpose in everything. She firmly believed everything happened for a reason. While she might not be able to figure out the reason, she still had a duty to take what had happened and make the best of things. If that meant serving out of her own abundance or blessing others in need when she had something to give, she would do it. God's Word said if she served even the least of those she encountered, she served as if unto Him. Meeting folks like Jacob and William was just a bonus.

seven

"Watch the ball, Jacob," William instructed his brother. "I might switch my pitch or drive it straight down the middle at you. But if you keep your eye on it, you'll be able to catch it no matter what."

"All right, Willie. I'm ready."

Jacob thumped his fist into his palm several times and assumed a rigid stance, poised on the balls of his feet. William smiled. He was ready. No doubt about it.

"Here it comes."

He wasn't sure why he gave his brother the warning. Jacob had already proven himself on more than one occasion to be an excellent catcher. His throws were getting stronger with each practice session they had together. It wouldn't be long before Jacob's skill with both bat and ball would exceed his own. Father joined them from time to time but admitted he didn't possess as great a skill at the game as his sons. So he stuck to instruction rather than actual play.

William could still remember the times he and his father had spent hours at the park near their old house throwing the ball back and forth to each other. Father had taught him and Jacob both how to hit. Not a bad legacy to pass down the line, even if Father spent more time correcting them than participating. William loved the chance today to work with his brother. They didn't often get the opportunity to make it to the old park and see Jacob's friends. Maybe once they rebuilt their holdings, they and Father could bat the ball to each other—for old time's sake.

"Are you going to throw it or not, Willie? My legs are getting tired from standing like this."

William shook his head. It looked as if he had let his thoughts wander. He gripped the ball in his hand and placed two fingers over the top, just like Father had once shown him. He cocked his arm back behind his head and prepared to release. Jacob would never know what hit him.

"Is this a boy's-only game, or can I watch as well?"

William let go of the ball just as Annabelle's voice reached his ears. He didn't have time to maintain a hold before it left his hand. His breath caught in his throat as the baseball zipped through the air toward Jacob.

God! Please let Jacob catch it.

Wait a minute. Had he just prayed? Yes, he had. And right now he needed the extra help.

A few seconds later, though, he realized he had no reason to worry. Jacob shifted his stance and caught the ball with ease, his grin beaming from ear to ear.

"I got it. I got it." The boy puffed out his chest. "See, Willie? I told you I could catch anything you threw!"

"Yes, I see that." William breathed a huge sigh of relief.

"Hi, Miss Annabelle." Jacob tossed the ball back and forth between his hands and approached. "When did you get here?"

Annabelle's soft laughter added a nice layer to the tense moment her sudden appearance caused. "I only just arrived." She reached out and ruffled the boy's fine blond hair. "In time to see you make that amazing catch."

Jacob puffed out his chest again. "That catch *was* amazing, wasn't it?"

"You did a fine job, Jacob." William turned to face Annabelle. "What brings you out to visit us today? You don't have a water bucket with you."

He held back the grimace at how callous his words sounded. Thankfully, Annabelle didn't seem to notice. Or if she did, she didn't show it.

"No, I took a quick break from meal preparations to come extend an invitation to you both."

"An invitation?" That sounded intriguing.

"You mean you want us to come somewhere with you?"

"Yes, Jacob." She looked back and forth between them. "And I am quite confident it's a place you both will love very much."

"Tell us! Tell us!" Jacob barely managed to contain his excitement. And he didn't even know where they might be going yet.

"Yes," William added. "By all means. Don't make us stand here and guess."

Instead of answering them, Annabelle reached into the pocket of her skirt and pulled out several identical items that looked like tickets of some sort.

"What are those?" He nodded at the items.

She extended her hand toward William. "Why don't you take a look and see for yourself?"

William held them in front of him to read what was printed. He gasped. How had she gotten ahold of these? Better yet, how had she known it would be like a dream come true to go?

"What are they, Willie?" Jacob took a step closer and craned his neck, trying to get a glimpse beyond William's hands. "Can I see? Can I? Please?"

William's voice caught in his throat. He opened his mouth several times and tried to speak. Nothing but air came out. Clearing his throat, he tried again.

"They're—" His voice cracked. He had to get it together. "They're tickets, Jacob," he managed, feeling like someone had landed a blow to his head.

"Tickets to what?"

"To a baseball game at Boulevard Park."

"A game?" Jacob sounded amazed. "A real, honest-to-goodness baseball game? With players and gloves and uniforms and everything?"

Annabelle laughed. "And everything, Jacob."

The sound of her voice broke through the cloud of disbelief surrounding William. "How did you manage this?"

"My father has a few connections with some rather influential people."

She spoke as if it wasn't a big deal. Then again, she likely had no idea just how important something like this was.

"I heard that the Western League had reorganized this year and that there was a club in the city that has established themselves as a charter member. Never in my wildest dreams did I think I'd actually be able to see the team play."

Annabelle shrugged. "Well, I remember another visit where you, Jacob, and your father were tossing and hitting the ball back and forth. I could see how much fun you were having and how much you seemed to love it. So I asked my father to make some inquiries. When he came back with the tickets, I could hardly wait to come here and give them to you."

"And your father didn't ask you why you had this sudden interest in baseball or why you needed three tickets?"

"Five, actually," she corrected.

"Five?" Who else was coming?

"Yes. In order to get these tickets I've given you, I also had to agree to bring my brother and sister as well."

"Oh." That didn't sound so bad. William figured it was more so she would have a chaperone. After all, he had yet to officially meet her parents, even if he was certain they knew about him. And that brought back the question about her father and the number of tickets. "You didn't say whether your father asked about the number of tickets."

"Yes, about that." She ducked her head, and a becoming blush spread across her cheeks. "He and my mother were rather curious when I gave your names, but I assured them the tickets were for two friends." She looked up at him, a pleading expression in her eyes. "I hope that was all right."

"We're your friends, Miss Annabelle," Jacob piped in before William could reply. "Of course it's all right."

William grinned and jerked a thumb toward his brother. "What he said."

"So you'll go then?"

As if he'd turn down an opportunity like this. He'd be daft to refuse. "Of course."

"Excellent." She took two steps backward. "Very well. I can't tarry much longer. I only came to make sure you wanted to come and to give you the tickets." Annabelle pointed toward the tent and tables off yonder. "Lunch will be served soon." She stepped away and turned.

"Will we meet you there?" The park was quite a ways from where they worked, but if they left early enough, they could make it in time.

"Oh, I hadn't thought about that." She glanced over her shoulder, pressed her lips into a thin line, and tilted her head. The way one corner of her mouth quirked, it made a dimple appear in her left cheek, giving her a pixieish quality. "Since we have to pass by here on our way, we'll take you in our carriage. Otherwise you'll have to walk quite a distance. And you might not make it in time."

A carriage. He hoped it wouldn't be enclosed. An open one suited them just fine. Dressed the way they'd be, the plainer the transportation the better. He didn't need to tell her that, though. Whatever carriage she sent would be fine with him.

"That sounds good."

"Very well." She nodded. "It appears to be all settled, then."

"Are we really going to a baseball game, Willie?"

"Yes, Jacob. And we have Miss Annabelle to thank."

"Thank you, lots and lots, Miss Annabelle. Willie talks about games all the time. We're going to have a great time. I just know it."

Annabelle ruffled the boy's hair again. "I certainly hope you do, Jacob. I hope you do."

Just before she turned to leave, William caught her eye and held her gaze. "Thank you," he said with all the sincerity he could muster. "You have no idea how much this means. . .to both of us."

A soft smile formed on her lips. "I believe I have some idea."

And with that, she left.

Four days. How in the world would he manage to wait that long?

❧

The park at the corner of East Lafayette and Helen was even larger than he imagined it would be for a team just getting on their feet again. Nothing like when the team in the city was the Wolverines, but every charter had to start somewhere. From what he'd heard, the owner was determined to make this team stick. They'd been without a professional team for almost six years. It was high time another one came back.

"Would you look at all the people, Willie!" Jacob ran ahead of them but not too far. "And the field. It's so big."

Annabelle walked right next to him. Matthew and Victoria ambled alongside her on her left. The carriage had arrived right after lunch. And just as he'd hoped, it wasn't enclosed. But another surprise came when the carriage deposited them at the nearest trolley stop and Matthew paid for their fares. He could accept that better than if Annabelle had covered them. From there they followed Jefferson to Helen and Helen to Lafayette.

"Annabelle tells me you and your brother really love the game of baseball." Matthew craned his neck forward to speak to him as they made their way to their seats. "Same here."

"Yes. A few years back, I followed everything I could read about the Wolverines, including the National League pennant and the exhibition championship they won seven years ago. Then the team disbanded, and Detroit has been minor league ever since. Until this year, that is."

"No kidding?" Matthew paused and moved to William's other side, no doubt to avoid talking around Annabelle and her sister. "Does this mean they're back at major league status again?"

"Not yet. They're only a charter member this year. But I have no doubt they'll be major league before too long. From what I've heard of their owner, George Vanderbeck, it's only a matter of time."

"Here we are," Annabelle announced as they reached the wooden benches where they'd sit.

William looked out at the playing field where the two teams were practicing and warming up for the game. It wasn't the best vantage point, but he couldn't complain. Just being here was the best gift he'd received in a long time. He ushered Jacob in first and made sure he got the seat closest to his brother. Matthew followed with Victoria and Annabelle bringing up the rear. The two girls immediately lapsed into a conversation all their own.

"So," Matthew continued once they were seated, "it appears you know far more than I about this game. What else do you know about this particular team?"

William almost laughed. He knew just about everything there was to know, short of being an actual member of the team. "What do you want to know?"

"Well, how about the players? Are any of them the same as when the Wolverines played in the city?"

"Not as far as I know. But then again, this is the first game I've attended, and this club is just getting started. I haven't heard much about who is playing on the team." He thought back to when the major league was there. "I do know that there was a high percentage of turnover during the eight years they played as the Wolverines. Only one member made it through all eight seasons, and that was Ned Hanlon."

"Hmm, I believe I heard his name once or twice."

"Well, you might not have heard much about baseball when it was here last. At least when it was worthy of front-page news."

Matthew nodded. "You've got a point there." He paused and looked out at the field. "What made them disband?"

"They didn't have enough fans to remain a major league team."

"Yes, I remember reading that Detroit was actually one of the smallest cities in the National League to have a baseball team."

"Right." William ticked off other cities on his fingers. "Boston, Chicago, Cleveland, and St. Louis all had thousands more fans than Detroit did. And since they couldn't keep up, they had to quit." He searched his memory for some other tidbits. "There were two attempts a few years ago to revive the team through the International League and the old Northwestern League."

Matthew chimed in. "But both ended after one season."

Annabelle's brother obviously had more than a rudimentary knowledge of the game. Perhaps they could have a rousing discussion today.

"Willie, look." Jacob tugged on his arm and pointed out at the field. "They're about to start. Come on. Let's watch."

William chuckled. "That's why we're here, Jacob. To watch. It would be hard not to."

His brother was so fixated on the field, he hadn't picked up on William's teasing. And that was just as well. The more enamored the lad was in the game, the less he'd have to be concerned with keeping an eye on him. He wouldn't likely get into too much trouble if he didn't take his eyes off the players.

Once the game began, the five of them watched everything with unabashed interest. William managed to glance out the corner of his eye to find Annabelle appearing to enjoy herself as well. At least the tickets proved worthwhile. He'd hate it if she went to all the trouble to get them and then didn't have a good time.

At several points in the game, Matthew demonstrated a true interest in baseball that almost mirrored William's. But he also had a lot of questions. William answered them all amid their banter on what they each knew. If he didn't miss his mark, he figured Matthew would become even more of a fan by the end of the day.

"You weren't kidding when you said you knew a lot about this game." Matthew shook his head. "I don't think it's possible to stump you."

William grinned. "Well, can I help it if I used to come to every game they played in town?"

"Wow! Every game? I only managed to make it to one or two."

"Well, you see, my father knew the owner, and our family had a standing invitation to the games. Since I loved it so much, we came."

He shifted his gaze to find Annabelle staring at him, her mouth parted slightly and her eyes registering surprise. Had he said something wrong? He tried to retrace his words. She spoke before he could put his finger on what caused her shock.

"Your father used to know the owner of the Wolverines?"

Ah, so that was what caught her attention. And she'd paid attention earlier when he had stated the old name of the team when they played at the major league level. Yes, he could see why such an admission would garner that type of reaction.

"Yes. They were good friends, in fact." No sense lying about it. She might as well know a bit more about his family's past. "Baseball has always been a favorite pastime of mine. When my father saw this, he managed to persuade the owner of the old team to allow us access to every game. We came every chance we could get."

"So what happened?" Annabelle leaned forward, her attention focused intently on him.

William shifted on the hard bench. A moment ago he thought it might be wise to share some details about his past. Now he wasn't so sure. It only brought back memories he'd much rather see remain buried. He'd been the one to open Pandora's box, though. Talking more about what his family once had wouldn't exactly unleash a swarm of evils upon them, but it would make him dwell on all they had lost.

"I'm not really sure," he finally managed. "Once the Wolverines disbanded, the owner seemed to disappear with them. A few others came and went with the attempts to start a team again during the years when we only had minor league status. But I never saw Mr. Stearns again."

"Do you think he might have left and moved to another city?" Matthew asked. "Maybe he switched to another team somewhere."

William hadn't thought of that, as it didn't happen too often with owners. "I suppose that's possible. All I know is my father never spoke of it, and I soon came to realize it was a mystery that wouldn't likely be solved anytime soon."

"That's so sad." Victoria sighed. "To think that a friendship like that could just fall apart. I mean, it sounds like he was an important person in your life when you were younger."

"Yes, he was." William had almost come to see him as part of the family. And then he was gone.

"It makes you wonder if there had been a disagreement of some sort." Annabelle tapped a finger to her lips as she often did when she became contemplative. "Or it's possible the disbanding of the team hit the owner really hard, and he wasn't able to handle it all."

"Well, whatever the reason, I only know I spent a lot of years wondering and waiting, hoping one day to see the return of a major league team." William extended his right arm toward the field. "Now it looks like I'll finally get that chance again."

Annabelle paused and licked her lips. She opened her mouth to speak then closed it, sitting back on the bench. "It does seem like that's a strong possibility."

Had she been about to say something else? William wasn't sure. But her remark seemed to put a period on that topic of conversation. No one else offered anything more, and their attention focused again on the game.

It was just as well. Talking about the past had made William a bit melancholy. Remembering what once was only made him question the reasons why again. They'd had everything.

Oh well. He didn't want to spoil a good thing by dwelling on the negatives today. Being at this game was a dream come true. And he intended to enjoy it.

eight

For several weeks following the baseball game, Annabelle devoted all of her spare time to assisting the farming families. So many of them had endeared themselves to her and found a special place in her heart. Most of all, she'd come to love the time she spent with the children.

The Cooper family had a little girl with a soft voice and a favorite doll that she took everywhere with her. When Annabelle had first brought water to them, Emily had tugged on her skirt to get her attention. Annabelle looked down to find a blond-haired girl of about three or four standing at her feet.

"Are you an angel?" Emily asked.

"No, I'm not. But I am doing what I feel God would like me to do." She set down the pail and squatted in front of the child. "My name is Annabelle Lawson. What's yours?"

"Emily Cooper." The girl stuck her thumb in her mouth and clutched her doll to her chest.

Her hair had been fashioned in two braids that draped across her shoulders, with flyaway strands framing her face and wispy bangs nearly hiding her dark blue eyes. Annabelle couldn't remember a more adorable child.

"And does your dolly have a name?"

Emily pulled her thumb from her mouth, glanced down at the doll, and offered a tentative smile. "Her name is Lizzie. And she's my best friend."

"It's important to have a best friend." Annabelle nodded. "You know she'll always be there with you. Make sure you're extra special nice to her, and if things get scary or hard, you

81

can talk to Lizzie."

"Mama says that, too." She peered up at Annabelle with a curious expression. "Are you a mama?"

Such innocence. It tugged at Annabelle's heart. "No, Emily. Not yet. But I will be someday, I hope. And when I am, I pray I have a little girl just like you." She flipped one of Emily's braids and touched her cheek.

"You'll be a good mama. I know. 'Cause bad mamas don't talk to girls like me. They're mean."

Unbidden tears formed in Annabelle's eyes. "Why, thank you for that, Emily. It was very sweet of you to say. And it means a lot to me."

"You're welcome." Emily reached out one arm and gave Annabelle a quick hug, crushing her doll between them. Then she pulled back. "I have to go now. Thank you for the water."

The little girl scampered off to play with some other children. Many more encounters had been similar to that one. Each one imprinted itself on Annabelle's memory and brought a smile each time she recalled it. From the rambunctious and mischievous Pennington boys who had unruly hair and a smattering of freckles across their faces, to the shy or hesitant kids who took a little bit to warm up to strangers— each one made her work that much more enjoyable.

She'd even started volunteering to watch the children under eight years old two days each week while their families and older siblings worked the fields. Thanks to the other women and some of the older children who came to visit, they had plenty of games for the children to play and books to read. Plus, one day a crate arrived full of slates, paper, chalk, and pencils.

They spent their days playing hopscotch, quoits, marbles, bilboquette, and pick-up sticks, or having fun with wooden building blocks. Some days they had races with rolling hoops and sticks to see who could get to the finish line first. When they weren't playing or reading, they sang songs and Annabelle kept watch while some of the children napped. It was such a rewarding time. Anything Annabelle could do to help keep their minds off the bleakness of their day-to-day lives, she'd do.

One afternoon Annabelle arrived and started to head for the main warehouse where the children stayed. But she heard her name being called and turned toward the voice.

"Miss Annabelle, come quick!" It was Mrs. Cooper, Emily's mother. The woman had worry written across her entire face, and she had obviously run all the way there.

"What's wrong, Mrs. Cooper?"

"It's Jacob Berringer," she said, trying to catch her breath. "He's been missing for over an hour. We can't find him anywhere."

Oh no! Not Jacob. William and his parents would be beside themselves. They no doubt already were.

"Well, what are we waiting for?" Annabelle hiked up her skirts, ready to run. "Let's go find him."

In no time at all, they gathered with the spontaneous search party that had been formed. Annabelle did a quick search of the faces, some familiar to her and some not. She caught sight of William and offered a smile with as much encouragement as she could. The elder Mr. Berringer stood next to him with his arm around his wife, who wrung her hands on the apron covering her simple working dress.

Annabelle hadn't officially met them, but there was no denying their identity.

"All right. Now that we've all gathered, let's split up to cover more ground." Mr. Pennington eyed the assemblage. "I suggest at least pairs, if not three or four to a group. But spread out and fan out from your assigned areas. We don't want to miss anything."

Mr. Pennington began making assignments. Annabelle waited to hear who would become her partner. Then all of a sudden William was standing next to her. She almost jumped when he touched her arm and spoke.

"Would you like to join my parents and me?" He made a loose gesture toward the others gathered. "I'm not sure how well you know the other workers, but we could use a fourth in our group."

Annabelle almost said she knew most of the ones who had come to help by name. If he wanted her to accompany them, though, she wouldn't turn him down. She didn't want to do or say anything that might make him change his mind. Perhaps it would give her a chance to get to know his parents better.

She smiled. "I'd like that very much."

He paused, and his expression took on a soft yet odd appearance. "Good. Follow me."

With a hand at her back—a gesture she'd never have imagined might come from him at a time like this—William led her around behind the others and brought her to stand in front of his parents.

"Father, Mother, I'd like to introduce you to Miss Annabelle Lawson. As you know, she dispenses water to the workers or stands at the food line on the days the hot meals are provided." He looked at Annabelle again with that softness in his eyes. "Miss Lawson, these are my parents, Daniel and Lucille Berringer."

Not a hint of superficial propriety existed in his tone. In fact, he seemed almost proud to introduce her. She wasn't sure if she should curtsy or simply incline her head. Mr. Berringer saved her the trouble though by extending his hand toward her.

"It's a pleasure to meet you, Miss Lawson. Jacob's spoken highly of you."

"Yes," added Mrs. Berringer. "Thank you so much for coming and offering your assistance to help find him."

"It's my pleasure, I assure you. Your son has become quite special to me. I'll do whatever I can to help."

Mr. Berringer flashed a quick glance and grin at William, who in turn looked at her then immediately back at his father with wide eyes and an almost imperceptible shake of his head. It took a moment for the silent communication to make sense. When realization dawned, heat rushed to her cheeks. She *had* meant the younger son, right?

"Very good," Mr. Berringer continued as if nothing was amiss. He looked over his shoulder to an area behind him. "We've already covered our plot, so we've been assigned the one adjoining ours. It starts here and goes to the northern edge of the property. Then it covers about seventy yards each to the east and the west."

"If each one of us takes a quadrant," William suggested, "we'll cover more area simultaneously."

"Yes, you're right, son. Let's do that." Mr. Berringer turned to his wife. "Lucille, why don't you take the east, and Miss Lawson, you can take the west. I'll cover the quadrant here to the south, and William, you take the part to the edge of our plot."

With their assignments made, each of them split in the four cardinal directions. Annabelle took each step carefully and looked up and down the many rows of vegetables. The others in the search party fanned out all around her. Some called Jacob's name, while others simply made their way through the various plots.

What had once been nothing more than an extensive, bare piece of land now thrived with rows and rows of fresh, green plants as far as the eye could see. From green beans and tomatoes to squash and the prime crop of potatoes, the workers had done a fine job of turning this property into a productive part of Mayor Pingree's potato patches.

It had been nearly three months since the first seeds were planted. Already the vines and roots showed signs of a substantial crop once everything could be harvested. If this land resembled the other plots throughout the city, it looked like the mayor's idea would be a grand success.

Annabelle stepped with caution across one row after another. She tried to stay within the cleared area surrounding the plants as much as possible. Could Jacob really be out here in the middle of the fields somewhere? If so, where would he be? She sent a silent prayer heavenward for God's angels to protect the young lad, wherever he was.

More than that, she prayed he hadn't been harmed in any way or somehow gotten lost. Detroit was a rather large city. Folks with less than honorable intentions existed everywhere. Oh, how she prayed something like that hadn't happened.

"Father," she said aloud. "Please guide our steps as we search for Jacob. You know where he is, Lord. I'm sure You have him under Your watchful eye. A lot of people here care about him and want to see him safe again with his family. I ask that You show us the way to find him so his parents can once again have their little boy safe and sound. In Your name, amen."

As soon as she finished, she crossed into yet another row of vegetables. This time staked tomato plants came up almost to her waist. Small green balls had formed on some of the vines. She was amazed to see the growth in such substantial amounts.

About halfway down the row, something caught her eye. From where she stood, it looked like an empty seed sack, but she couldn't tell. Pivoting on her heel, she almost lost her balance and tumbled onto a few plants. After she righted herself, Annabelle took careful steps toward the object in question.

"Oh my!"

She covered her mouth with her hand. Then she giggled as she looked down upon the angelic sleeping form of Jacob Berringer. Curled up near one of the tomato plants and using a seed sack for a pillow, he rested his head on his arm and appeared to be lost in dreamland. He looked so peaceful that she didn't want to disturb him. But his parents and brother were worried. She had no choice.

Annabelle knelt beside the boy and placed a hand on his shoulder.

"Jacob," she called in a soft voice. "Jacob. Wake up."

He mumbled and curled his legs tighter against his body, bunching up the seed sack under his head.

"Jacob," she said again, only louder.

This time he smacked his lips together as his eyelids fluttered several times. Annabelle put pressure on his shoulder again. After a few seconds, his eyes opened, and he squinted under the bright sun. She shifted so her shadow would cover him. When he was able to focus, he gave her a sleepy grin.

"Hi, Miss Annabelle. Where did you come from?"

Poor thing. He didn't even seem to be aware he'd fallen asleep in the middle of the field.

"Hello there, Jacob. I was walking up and down these rows of vegetables, and I found you asleep in the middle of them."

Jacob sat up with a start and looked around. He reached up and ran a hand through his hair, making the sleep-rumpled locks even more of a mess.

"You mean I've been sleeping here?"

The incredulous look he gave her elicited another giggle. "Yes, and you've caused a lot of people to be out looking for you. Come on." She reached out her hands and took hold of his as she stood, pulling him up with her. "Let's get you back to your parents so they can call off the search. They'll be happy to know you're all right."

He dragged his feet a bit as he followed, and his head remained downcast. "I'm sorry, Miss Annabelle," he mumbled. "I didn't mean to scare anyone."

Annabelle tousled his hair and draped an arm around his shoulders. "It's all right, Jacob. Everything will be fine when they see you're safe and sound again. You'll see."

Everything *was* all right. Just as Annabelle had predicted. Mr. and Mrs. Berringer threw their arms around their youngest son, showering him with affection and words of reassurance. William also showed his happiness to see his brother back with a mock punch to his cheek. Several of the volunteers from the search party heard the commotion and came to investigate.

"It's all right. We've found him," Mr. Berringer announced. "Spread the word. And thank you so much for your help."

In no time at all, everyone dispersed and went back to their duties. Annabelle watched the tender family reunion and felt like an outsider. She slowly took a few steps backward. It would be best if she just slipped away unnoticed and returned to the other children.

Mrs. Berringer looked up before she could escape.

"Oh, Miss Lawson. We were just about to partake of our noonday meal when we noticed Jacob was missing. We'd like to invite you to join us." She paused and looked to her husband, who nodded. "That is, if you don't have somewhere else you need to be."

"We also want to thank you for taking time to find our boy," Mr. Berringer added.

Annabelle looked at Jacob's parents; then she glanced at William. His face showed a spark of interest and perhaps even eagerness, but he didn't say anything. Well, she couldn't count on him for help in deciding. So she shifted her focus to Jacob. His wide smile and the way he nodded his head up and down in rapid succession gave her more than enough reason to stay. Now why couldn't William be that transparent?

"Very well," she finally said. "I accept your generous offer."

"Splendid." Mr. Berringer roped Jacob with his arm and pulled his son close as he wrapped his other arm around his wife and led the way toward a makeshift encampment. It was simple yet functional.

William hung back and allowed her to precede him as they followed his family, his hand again barely touching the small of her back. She couldn't tell if he was just being a gentleman or if it meant something more. Mrs. Berringer immediately set about stirring the stew that had been set back away from the fire. It smelled delicious, and Annabelle's stomach rumbled in response.

Jacob laughed. "I guess you're hungry, too, huh, Miss Annabelle?"

She placed her hand over her abdomen as her cheeks warmed. "Yes, Jacob. It appears I am."

"Well, don't worry," Mrs. Berringer said without looking up. "We will have hot stew in a matter of moments. It's not as nice as the meals you and the other ladies provide, but—"

"I'm sure it will be delicious," Annabelle rushed to assure her.

A few horse blankets had been spread out on the ground to cover the dirt. Jacob tugged on her sleeve for her to sit next to him, so she obliged. William lowered himself on her other side, taking pains to maintain a respectful distance. His actions seemed so contradictory, and his silence didn't help, either.

Once the bowls were filled and passed around, Mr. Berringer bowed his head, and his family followed suit. Just before she closed her eyes, she glanced at William, whose eyes remained open.

He was in so much pain and so confused. She wished she could come up with the answers that would ease his troubled mind and set him back on the course toward faith once more.

It wasn't up to her, though. She could only be a friend and continue to share God's love any way she knew how.

Once the simple prayer ended, the family all dug into their late lunch. Annabelle raised her spoon to her lips for her first taste. Amazed to find chunks of meat mixed with vegetables amid a seasoned, thick, gravylike base, she swallowed it all and eagerly dipped her spoon for another bite.

"We are so blessed to have such generous families working alongside us each day," Mrs. Berringer said between bites.

Mr. Berringer set his spoon in his bowl and looked up. "Whenever extras of anything are discovered, most of the families share from their abundance. One of the older sons works for a meat shop in the city and managed to secure a donation from the shop owner," he went on to explain. "Thanks to that, we've been able to make a meal from the portion given to us on more than one occasion."

"It's not much," Mrs. Berringer continued, "but it fills our stomachs and gives us strength to keep working."

"Stew is my favorite." Jacob spoke with his mouth full and received a silent reprimand from his mother. He swallowed and gave everyone a sheepish grin. "Sorry."

"It's delicious," Annabelle said, taking another generous bite to prove her declaration. "I haven't tasted stew this good since I don't remember when."

The compliment made William's mother brighten and sit up straighter. "If nothing else, being without has caused us to rethink our priorities and determine what is truly important in life." She sighed. "I'm afraid we once placed money and prestige above the blessings our heavenly Father had provided. But now. . ." She let her voice trail off as she ate another spoonful of stew.

"We're not saying we didn't appreciate what God had given us," Mr. Berringer rushed to add. "We're just saying our current situation has given us a fresh outlook on life. I'm confident we'll again establish ourselves, but for now I'm thankful we have work to do and a place to live." A frown formed on his lips, and his eyes filled with sorrow. "I'm afraid others didn't fare as well."

Annabelle was impressed with their positive attitudes, despite all they'd lost. For the first time, she had a glimpse of what life had been like for William prior to the panic last year. Although he seemed to have turned his back right now on the faith that he'd been taught or even believed, at least he still had his family to support him.

"I know exactly what you mean," she said. "Seeing so many in need has given me new insight into how I can follow the commandment to love my neighbors as myself." She wiped her mouth. "I dearly love what I'm able to do and the wonderful people I've met as a result."

Mrs. Berringer's eyes sparkled with a sheen of moisture. "It's thanks to your willing service that we have the strength to push through the tough times no matter what."

Annabelle didn't know how to respond, so she smiled softly and nodded. The Berringers had quite a legacy built around them. Despite their recent loss, they maintained their faith and continued to be a light amid the dark circumstances surrounding the city. They had many reasons to be proud of the paths they now chose. If only William could see the benefit in continuing to trust God, even through the storms.

She looked at him for a moment only to see he kept his head down and focused on his bowl. He hadn't participated at all, but at least he hadn't gotten up or walked away. Annabelle prayed he listened to what his parents had said. Perhaps their words could serve as water to the seeds she'd planted a few weeks ago. The foundation was there in his life. She could see that. He just needed time.

God had brought them into her life and her into theirs. Nothing happened without a purpose. Annabelle looked forward to seeing how it all played out.

nine

"Where are we headed first?"

William walked alongside his father on a Sunday afternoon a week later as they ventured into some of the more affluent areas of the city. Even though they both had taken great care with their grooming that morning and wore some of their better Sunday clothing, he still felt shabby and insignificant. It didn't matter that they might look the part. Inside he didn't feel it.

His father looked down at a piece of paper where he'd scribbled some names and addresses. "We'll pay a visit to Amos Shepherd."

"Are you sure these men won't mind us barging in like this? I mean, we didn't exactly notify them in advance that we'd be coming. There was a time when we'd leave a calling card first."

Father sighed. "Yes, I know. However, we don't have the luxury of planning ahead like we once did. We have no other choice but to seize the opportunities as they arise. And that means today."

William wasn't quite sure he could grab hold of the same determination or zeal his father had managed to find, but he'd do his best. It couldn't be easy for a man like Father to resort to this. They were asking for special favors, plain and simple. A dozen scenarios played out in his head about how they'd be received by those who had once openly welcomed them into their homes. He only hoped the worst of them wouldn't come true today.

Walking up the six steps to the front door of the Shepherd

home, William noted that the windowpanes lacked their former decor. It appeared as if Amos and his family might have been affected as well.

A moment or two after Father knocked, the latch clicked and the door swung open.

"Good afternoon," the butler said in a formal tone, eyeing them both from head to toe with disdain in his eyes. "How may I help you?"

They still were able to afford their butler? Perhaps they weren't as affected as William had thought.

"We are here to see Mr. Shepherd," Father replied. "You may tell him that Daniel and William Berringer have come to call."

A barely perceptible nod on an almost emotionless face was the only sign that the man had even heard them. He stepped back to allow them entrance.

"You may wait in the sitting room," the man instructed as he closed the door behind them. "I shall inform Mr. Shepherd immediately."

William and his father made their way into the front room and took a seat in opposite chairs facing the windows. They had a clear view of the doorway so they'd know when Amos appeared. Two minutes later, the sound of shoes clicking on the hardwood floor in the entry preceded Mr. Shepherd's arrival.

"Daniel!" Amos stepped into the room, aided by a polished beech wood cane with a brass handle. His slicked back, silver-lined hair and tailored suit made him appear every bit the dapper gentleman. "I must admit, your presence this afternoon is quite a surprise."

William didn't like the forced jovial sound to the man's voice, nor the reserved smile that didn't quite reach his eyes. Nevertheless, he and his father stood to shake hands with Shepherd as etiquette demanded.

"Yes, my friend. And I apologize for arriving unannounced."

Shepherd dismissed Father's comment with a wave of his hand. "Nonsense. You are always welcome in my home." He hooked his thumbs on the pockets of his vest and rocked back on his heels. "So tell me. What brings you here today?"

William took a tiny step back to allow his father to control the conversation. He was only there for moral support and to plead his own case if it became necessary.

"Well," his father began, "this isn't the easiest thing for me to do."

Shepherd moved toward a wingback chair. "Please," he invited, "sit down, and start from the beginning."

After they sat, Amos perched on the edge of his chair, one leg extended out in front of him while the other remained bent at a perpendicular angle.

Father cleared his throat. "I'm sure you're well aware of the effect the crisis had on my family."

"Yes, and I'm sorry I haven't been in touch lately to extend my condolences. So many of our previous acquaintances have lost so much."

"We've made out better than some. That much is certain." Father took a deep breath. "We're here today to ask if there is anything at all with which you're aware for either myself or William to do in order to get back on our feet. You're well acquainted with our work habits and our ingenuity. We're not afraid of starting small to begin, either."

Shepherd started to respond, but Father continued.

"I know you might not have anything yourself. But if you know of someone who does, we'd be appreciative of your direction or even a good word on our behalf."

William watched Shepherd with a wary eye. Something about the man's demeanor didn't sit right. He went through all the motions of appearing to consider Father's request, but his actions and his facial expression didn't seem to line up.

"Daniel, you know me as well as anyone. If I had any resources at all at my disposal, I'd be the first in line to open any doors I could for those who needed it."

Here it comes. William tried not to roll his eyes at the predictable response from someone who didn't want to exert any effort toward helping someone who had fallen on hard times as his father had.

"However, although we fared measurably better than others, the current economic situation has not looked favorably upon us, either. We are barely managing to make ends meet. Two of my associates and I are working long hours at the bank in an attempt to find anything extra from which we can pull to help ease the city's burden." He sighed. "Most simply aren't able to afford additional help at this point."

The words were delivered with just the right measure of regret and sympathy, but William still wasn't convinced of the man's sincerity. Call it a hunch. He just didn't believe him.

"I understand," Father said with a note of obvious resignation. "We weren't certain what the result would be of our efforts today. If there is anything out there, we're going to find it, though."

Shepherd leaned on his cane and rose. Father and William did the same.

"I do appreciate you taking time out of your day off to see us." Father extended his hand, which Shepherd took.

"Of course. It was my pleasure."

"And if you do hear of anything, or if circumstances change in any way, be sure to come find us at the Lawson plot to the north."

The man rested both hands on the handle of his cane and nodded. "Of course. Of course. You know I will."

Father took a step toward the front door. "We'll see ourselves out."

"It was good seeing you again, Daniel. Give my best to

your wife and young son."

William followed behind his father and gave Shepherd a polite dip of his head in farewell. "Thank you, sir."

"William," he returned.

Once they closed the door behind them and descended the steps, William had to bite his tongue to keep from speaking aloud his thoughts regarding Shepherd. From the moment the man had entered the room, William knew what the end result would be. He and his father were begging. There was no other way to put it. Accepting assistance freely offered was one thing. Seeking it out in this manner was quite another. It went against everything inside him. Still, his father needed his support. He'd give it no matter what.

"All right," his father said with a bravado William was sure he didn't feel, "that didn't turn up any possibilities. Let's move to the next one on our list."

It pained him to see his father reduced to this. What else could they do, though? Fighting back was the only solution. If they accepted their fate and did nothing about it, they'd be right where they were for years to come.

"Whom do you have written down for our second visit?" William nodded his head toward the paper his father held.

Father consulted the list of names. "Samuel Jacobson." He looked down the street from where they stood. "That's only two blocks away."

"Let's get moving, then. We don't have all afternoon." William gave his father a grin he hoped would be an encouragement. "The sooner we make it through that list of names, the sooner we can return to Mother and Jacob, perhaps even with some good news."

"You're absolutely right, my boy." Father clapped him on his back with a solid thump. "Time's a wasting."

Fifteen minutes later, they were back on the sidewalk again. That visit hadn't gone much better than the first.

Jacobson didn't even invite them past the foyer. He at least waited to hear what they had come to ask before hastily interrupting to tell them he had no answers for them. Based on how eager he seemed to see them leave, William could tell those doors wouldn't be open for them anytime soon.

So they crossed off that name and moved to the one in the third spot. That meeting lasted less than three minutes, and this time they weren't even invited into the house.

After three hours and eleven different stops, they still had no offers extended and no opportunities available. With each door that closed behind them or in their faces, William watched the position of his father's shoulders fall lower and lower. A man who had started out the day with a spring in his step and expectation in his eyes now stood next to him with the light dimmed and his feet dragging. Hopelessness had definitely begun to seep into his demeanor.

Placing a comforting arm around the man who had been a rock for as long as he could remember, William forced as much encouragement into his voice as he could muster.

"Well, we seem to be striking out today, that's for sure." He chuckled, but it sounded hollow. "We're not giving up, though, right? I mean, since when have the Berringer men taken defeat lightly?"

His father offered a grin that came out looking more like a grimace. "Never," he said without conviction or emotion.

"Right." William thumped his fist into his palm. "So we won't start now." He searched his memory for some of the inspiring advice his father had given him growing up. "You've always said that God is watching out for us. That He has our best interests at heart."

Father nodded. "I have at that."

"So that means there's still a chance out there somewhere that something will break in our favor. Just because we didn't have success from one afternoon, that doesn't mean we're down for the count. We'll just reorganize, rethink our plan, and start again next weekend."

It broke William's heart to see his father in such a state. What had he honestly expected from today, though? Surely he didn't think they'd solve their entire financial future with just a few visits to the homes of previous business associates. It couldn't be easy, though, calling on the men once considered trusted confidants, only to have them turn their backs on sincere pleas for help. He just hoped his words didn't sound as false to his father as they did to his own ears.

A long sigh escaped from Father's lips before he looked at William. "Thank you, son. It means a lot to me to have your support. I might not be the best company right now, but having you here beside me makes all the difference. If you hadn't come along, I might have given up after the first few stops."

William wished he deserved the praise his father bestowed upon him. He felt like such a hypocrite, spouting off words he himself was only recently coming to believe so that he could offer what reassurance he could to a man who needed to hear them. Perhaps William needed to hear them, too.

"Why don't we call it a day and head back to the farm plot?"

"I think that's an excellent idea," William agreed. "Maybe tomorrow we'll have another idea." At least he hoped so.

❧

"Am I doing it right, Willie?"

Jacob stood at the edge of the pond at the far end of the farming land, holding a fishing pole so tightly that his knuckles had turned white.

William had to laugh. "Yes, you are, Jacob, but remember to loosen your grip on the pole. If a fish bites, you'll be too tense to reel it in properly."

"Oh," was all his brother said. He did adjust his stance and his clasp, though.

About twenty feet away, William had his own line cast into the murky waters. If they had any luck today, maybe they could cook up some fresh fish for dinner.

"Have you caught anything yet?"

William started at the sound of Annabelle's voice and jerked his head to see her approach from behind him. With her hair pinned atop her head and her clothes pressed free of wrinkles, she looked the very picture of elegance. Still, he couldn't deny the breath of fresh air she brought to an otherwise wearisome day.

"Not yet, no," he answered her. "Between the two of us, though, we're hoping for something."

"I hope you don't mind my coming. Your mother told me I could find you here."

He shrugged. "Not at all. Did you have something on your mind?"

"Not particularly, but after speaking with your mother for a few minutes, I learned about the visits you and your father paid to some old friends yesterday."

Friends? If you could call them that. From the way they treated his father, he'd be more likely to call them enemies or adversaries. "Yes, we were looking to see if things had improved yet in the various financial markets. I thought it might be too soon, but Father wanted to try anyway."

"You never know with things like money. From all appearances, the situation might appear bleak, but there could be a tiny crack that leads to something more." She stepped into the peripheral line of his vision. "You just have to find the crack."

"We didn't have much luck at that yesterday. And I have a feeling it took quite a toll on my father."

The words were out of his mouth before he realized it. Why was he admitting something like that to Annabelle? She didn't need to hear about their failures. It wasn't as if she could do anything anyway.

"How so?"

Now he'd done it. He'd opened the door, and she'd stepped right in. In truth, what could it hurt?

"When you try again and again for something only to have the door slammed in your face, it gets to you after a while."

She nodded. "I can understand that. He isn't giving up, though, is he?"

William cast a quick glance at her to see concern etched across her delicate features. He warmed at the thought that she cared enough to ask.

"No, but I've never seen him so dejected. He's always been the strength of our family, and yesterday I watched each refusal weaken his resolve."

"Still, the fact that he even took the chance of doing what he did speaks of great inner strength. If the results were as bad as they seem from what you've said, it's bound to take its toll on anyone. I admire you both for even trying."

He reeled in his line, adjusted the lure, and recast. "I told my father that the Berringer men don't give up easily. He agreed that we just have to try again."

"And you're absolutely right. One day doesn't represent the full extent of opportunities. You'll find the right door soon enough. I'm sure of it."

"Yes, but how soon?" A tinge of anger found its way into his voice. "We paid a visit to almost a dozen different people who were supposed to be friends of my father. Not a single one offered any hope whatsoever." He'd been a comfort to his father yesterday. Today, though, he wasn't in the mood to pretend. "What makes you think any future attempts will yield different results?"

"Because I know God rewards the diligent," she said simply.

"Then why are we stuck here working as farmers when

we spent years being industrious and conscientious enough for three families? Why are we being forced to pay the price for others' mistakes and lapses in judgment? How did we get selected to be among those who have to bear the brunt of the financial depression instead of the ones who are responsible for the economic downfall?"

Shock appeared on Annabelle's face at his rant, and her mouth fell open slightly. He almost rushed to apologize, to erase that hint of hurt on her face and bring back a smile, but he didn't have it in him.

"I—" She swallowed twice as she seemed to struggle finding the words to say.

"Look, Miss Lawson," he began, softening his words. "I appreciate your attempts to infuse a measure of hope into an otherwise hopeless situation. The fact of the matter is that you truly don't have any answers. So let's forget about trying to paint a rosy picture, all right?" He groaned and looked away from her.

That hadn't come out as he'd wanted it to. Discouraging her completely was not what he had in mind. He enjoyed her company too much to dismiss her or risk losing her interest. She'd managed to temper his anger more than once and helped him see he wasn't alone in this. He tried again.

"I do appreciate your concern, but if you don't mind, I think I just need some time alone."

William still didn't like how selfish he sounded. Maybe Annabelle wouldn't take any of this personally.

"Very well, Mr. Berringer." She interlocked her fingers in front of her for a moment. "I'll leave you to your solitude. . .for now."

He looked at her.

"Don't expect it to last forever, though. In the meantime, I'll be praying you either find a solution or a way to make peace with the way things are." She turned on her heel and called over her shoulder. "I hope you catch something. You or Jacob."

William watched her leave. Good thing Jacob seemed to be preoccupied with his own pole and fishing, or he might have gotten upset that William had sent Annabelle away like that. He silently rebuked himself for not asking her to stay and for his attitude. Something about her caused him to act far from his norm. He could generally keep his emotions under control. With Annabelle, though, and the more time they spent together, staying in control became harder and harder. Had she stayed any longer, he might have said something he'd regret or even done something impulsive like asked her to take a walk with him.

Now where had that come from? One moment he was upset about the results of yesterday's visits, and the next he was thinking about taking afternoon strolls with her. Annabelle affected him like no other young woman had. She was gone, though, and he could again get back to the matter at hand—catching something for dinner. There was time later to dwell on his feelings for Miss Lawson, whatever they were.

ten

"Come in, Annabelle. Come in," her father beckoned when she knocked on the open door to his study.

She stepped inside the dark interior and wrung her hands together. "I'm sorry to disturb you, Father, but there is a matter of great importance I wish to discuss with you."

He looked up from the ledger he was reading and quirked an eyebrow. "It sounds serious." Leaning back in his chair, an amused expression crossed his face. "I don't wish to cause my daughter distress, so why don't you take a seat and we'll have ourselves a little chat?"

Good. She had hoped Father would be willing to see her now instead of putting it off to a later date. From what she'd gleaned after talking with William yesterday, he and his father could use a little spark of hope in their plight.

"Now tell me what this is all about. I'll see if I can't help erase that look of concern from that beautiful face."

Perched on the edge of the padded leather chair opposite her father's mahogany desk, the two options for presenting her request came to mind. Licking her lips, she chose straightforward and direct.

"Father, you know I've been volunteering a good portion of my time at the land you donated for the workers to farm."

He nodded. "Yes. Go on."

"I love everything I do there. The families I've met, the children I've supervised. It's been an incredible blessing to have the chance to get involved in their lives in such an intimate manner."

Her father pressed his lips together for a second or two

and regarded her. "Something tells me there is an exception coming. Perhaps involving one particular family or something else for the children, such as more slates?"

She should have known he would ascertain her reason for coming before she got around to saying it. He didn't hold commanding positions in several operations by being oblivious to the needs or opportunities around him.

"Yes, there is one family I have gotten to know quite well—the Berringers. A father, mother, and two sons," she explained. "Their dedication and hard work ethic have impressed me a great deal, not to mention the sustaining faith of Mr. and Mrs. Berringer, despite all that's happened in their lives recently."

Father leaned forward and propped his elbows on the edge of his desk. "So where do I come in? How might I be of assistance?"

"Yesterday I paid them a visit and learned that the oldest son, William, and his father had spent a substantial amount of time Sunday afternoon visiting old associates and friends from before the financial devastation."

"Hmm. I would hazard a guess that they didn't exactly get the reception they'd hoped for."

She sighed. That was putting it mildly. She wasn't there, but she could tell from William's face and tone that it hadn't gone well at all. "No. In fact, they had no success whatsoever. They were only making inquiries to see if any opportunities existed anywhere for them to get their feet back in the door. Only they returned empty-handed."

"Times are tough for everyone, Annabelle. I know you're aware of this." He steepled his fingers. "Still, that's no reason for previous friends to turn their backs on someone simply because a family has fallen on hard times."

"That's exactly what I thought." Annabelle was grateful her father seemed to be seeing things the same way. "That's also why I've come. To see if you might be able to help in some way." Before he could respond, she rushed on. "I know you can't guarantee anything, but if you could just make a few inquiries of your own and test the waters, it could be a start."

"Do you know anything specific about this family? Perhaps what the father or son were doing before last year?"

Thinking back to the conversations she'd had with William, she tried to recall if he'd mentioned any specifics.

"I believe they were connected to the railroads at the investment level and in manufacturing, but I'm not sure."

"And you say their last name is Berringer?"

"Yes. Daniel Berringer is the father."

Father nodded. "That will help a great deal. I'm sure I can find out exactly what he did and where he was working before."

Her breath caught, and she inhaled a sharp breath. "Does that mean you'd be willing to assist them?"

Removing his elbows from the edge, he folded his arms on the desk and splayed out his hands. "I can't make any promises, but I will promise to do my best to exhaust my contacts and uncover the potential opportunities beneath every rock I find. . .no matter how small," he added with a grin and a wink.

She grinned as well and stood. When he rose from his chair, she came around the desk and threw her arms around his neck, burying her head against his chest and inhaling the blended scents of peppermint and tobacco.

"Thank you so much, Father."

He wrapped his arms around her and returned the hug. "You're more than welcome, little one. Anything I can do for my favorite daughter."

Annabelle pulled back and looked up into his teasing eyes. She lowered her arms and planted her fists on her hips. "Well, I *am* your first. I *should* be your favorite." Lowering her voice, she added, "Let's not tell Victoria, though."

He chuckled. "I agree. That would be quite unwise."

"I'm not so little anymore, either."

A melancholic expression crossed his face. "No, you're not." He reached out and touched her cheek. "My little girl is all grown up, right before my eyes." His eyes narrowed as he looked down at her. "So how old is this oldest son in the Berringer family?"

Annabelle looked off to the left. "Umm, I believe he's twenty-three. Why?"

Father stepped away and back behind his desk, where he reached for the ledger he'd been reviewing when she'd arrived. "Mere curiosity is all."

Something about his mannerisms told Annabelle there was more to it than that. He and Mother had no doubt talked about William, but they had yet to say anything to her. Maybe they didn't mind her spending so much time with him.

"All right." She finally shrugged. "Is there any other information you need from me?"

"Not at the moment, no." He glanced down at the book in his hands. "But could you go find your mother and tell her I'd like to speak with her, please?"

She was going to ask if she could tell Mother the reason for the request, but that was none of her business. She'd simply do as Father asked.

"I'll tell her straightaway," she said as she moved toward the hallway.

"Thank you," he said without looking up.

❧

"Afternoon, Miss Annabelle." Jacob greeted her as soon as she approached the section of rows he and William were tending.

"Good afternoon. Are your parents nearby?"

William turned his head and looked up from his kneeling position beside a tomato plant. He plucked off a few tomatoes with black rotting on the bottom and removed what appeared to be wormlike creatures from the stems.

"They're about ten rows over."

Annabelle stepped closer and peered into the pail where he tossed the worms. Their green bodies blended so well with the plants, she was amazed he could even spot them.

"What are those?"

"Hornworms," William answered. "They feed on the leaves and tomatoes during the day, and they are so well camouflaged, it is hard to see them. We've also found them on some of the potatoes, peppers, and eggplant."

She wrinkled her nose and stepped back. "Do they cause a big problem?"

"They can. There usually aren't too many hanging around. If we don't catch them now, when they become adults, they turn into moths and eat the leaves."

"Here, I've got one, Miss Annabelle. Wanna see?"

She turned and came face-to-face with a fat, four-inch caterpillar that Jacob held up to her. Concealing a shriek as she stumbled backward, Annabelle slapped her hand over her heart. "Gracious, no!"

William laughed out loud and returned his attention to his task. "They're actually quite harmless to us."

"Be that as it may," she began, "I still have no desire to have any further surprise meetings with them."

"What is it you've come to speak to my parents about?"

She kept a wary eye on Jacob and cautiously approached the two of them again. There was no telling what other surprises he might have hiding nearby. She determined to keep the boy within her sight. Glancing out the corner of her eye, she turned again toward William.

"My family is going to be spending Sunday afternoon on

Belle Isle. I came to ask if your family would like to join us. You'll be invited to Sunday services as well."

"Oh." He didn't make eye contact with her in any way, instead remaining focused on his task. "Yes, that's something you'll need to ask them. I'm not sure what they might have planned for that day—if anything."

She had a feeling his lackluster response had to do with the mention of church more than the idea of spending a day relaxing with a lot of other families. That was fine. He didn't have to show great enthusiasm about her invitation. But she did hope he would come.

"You said they're working ten rows away?"

"Yes. To the north." William pointed in front of him.

Annabelle rose up on the balls of her feet and peered through the plants. Mr. and Mrs. Berringer were crouched low, like William and Jacob.

"Thank you. I'll leave you two to your work and go speak with them." Gathering her skirt in her hands, she stepped sideways through the first row of plants. "Have fun."

Neither one of them responded. She didn't expect them to, either. As she headed toward Mr. and Mrs. Berringer, she couldn't resist a peek at the plants to see if she could spot any of those worms herself. It took her searching four different plants before she finally found one. William was right. Those critters were quite adept at disguising themselves. Thankfully, her volunteer work didn't involve that task. She'd never be able to handle it.

After making her way through several more rows, she came upon Mr. and Mrs. Berringer kneeling in front of the stalks and leaves much like William had been. Mrs. Berringer looked up when Annabelle kicked a dislodged rock in her path.

"Miss Lawson, how good it is to see you today."

"Good afternoon, Mrs. Berringer. Mr. Berringer," she added with a nod at the man only a few feet farther down the row. "I just spoke with your sons, and they told me where I might find you."

Lucille shielded her eyes and peered up at her. "Was there something in particular you needed? Forgive me for not greeting you properly, but I'm afraid my hands are rather soiled," she said as she gave her hands a self-conscious swipe through her apron. "As are my clothes. I don't wish for any of that to get on you."

Annabelle waved off the excuse. "No, no. It's fine, I assure you. Don't feel the need to rise on my account. I only came to extend an invitation to you and your family for this coming Sunday."

"An invitation?" Her expression changed to one of piqued interest. "To where, might I ask?"

"My mother came to me yesterday and mentioned there would be several families gathering on Belle Isle to enjoy our day of rest. She suggested that it might be a refreshing change of pace for all of you, and I offered to come personally to tell you about it."

"Belle Isle?" Mr. Berringer spoke from beyond his wife's shoulder. "That's a popular place for many affluent families here in the city."

"The very same." Annabelle nodded. "There is a host of activities for everyone to enjoy. I know William and Jacob like to go fishing, so they could bring their poles. And there are the paths for taking leisurely strolls or areas where we'll be setting up a picnic. We're praying the weather cooperates and remains as nice as it's been lately."

Mrs. Berringer hadn't protested or refused yet, so Annabelle continued.

"We usually attend services in the morning at Memorial Chapel near Jefferson. We'd be especially honored if you would join us there first. Then we can all venture together to Belle Isle."

Mrs. Berringer looked down at her clothing with a grimace. "We still have our Sunday outfits, but we are sure to attract far more attention than I would be comfortable with, especially among those who knew us before. . ." She trailed off.

Annabelle silently scolded herself for not thinking of that. She should have known appearance would be of prime concern when mingling with others at a social event, whether it be church or a picnic.

"Nonsense," she rushed to reassure the woman. "There are many families who attend each week who are dressed exactly as you are now. Some own only two outfits. Others come dressed in finer clothing, but I can state with absolute certainty that you will not stand out in any way nor draw any unnecessary attention by your presence."

Mrs. Berringer shifted and looked over her shoulder at her husband. Annabelle couldn't see the woman's face, but by the shrug Mr. Berringer gave her, she assumed the silent conversation the two shared meant an acceptance would be forthcoming.

Lucille turned again to face Annabelle. "Miss Lawson, thank you so much for taking the time to come and invite us. We would be both pleased and honored to join you and your family this coming Sunday." A soft smile formed on her lips, and the sheen of tears appeared in her eyes. "Is there anything I might bring?"

Annabelle made a mental note to thank her mother for the foresight regarding the picnic items they'd be providing. "No, nothing. Our cook, Katie, is going to be preparing a feast that is sure to delight, so you needn't worry about the food. And there is sure to be a variety of games being played throughout the afternoon. I'm certain the other families will provide the essentials there." She smiled. "You just come with your family, and everything else will be taken care of."

"Thank you," the woman managed beyond a catch in her throat.

The look of appreciation Mrs. Berringer bestowed upon her meant more than any words could say. And the soft thanks she spoke said everything necessary.

"You are more than welcome. Mother will be pleased to hear of your acceptance. I'll hurry home to tell her the good news." Annabelle started to leave then turned and stepped forward, placing a hand on Mrs. Berringer's shoulder. "You won't regret it. I promise."

"I'm sure we won't. And thank you again. The good Lord surely has sent many angels to us this season."

Annabelle only responded with a smile before taking her leave. Funny that Mrs. Berringer should mention angels. She didn't feel like one, even if others saw her in that manner. One thing she did know, though. God truly was at work here.

eleven

"Regardless of where you are now or what has happened, God has not forgotten you."

William repeated that line from the pastor in his head over and over again on the ferry ride over to Belle Isle. When the invitation to join Annabelle's family also included a visit to church, he wanted to make his excuses not to attend. However, they were being gracious by even associating with his family. At the very least, he could be cordial.

The rhythmic dips and plunges of the ferry on the water sent his mind back to the sermon from that morning. The pastor had a way of taking his listeners to a low and contemplative state by reminding them they were but specks compared to the mighty and powerful God. Then he'd raise their hopes and faith by promising God knew each and every one of them by name.

"Are not five sparrows sold for two farthings, and not one of them is forgotten before God? But even the very hairs of your head are all numbered. Fear not therefore: ye are of more value than many sparrows."

He'd heard scripture verses such as that one for years growing up. Even Annabelle had used a similar comparison as a way to remind him that the struggles he and his family now faced were not missed by God. Yet for all the promises he'd been told and all the reassurances he'd been given, he still had trouble determining the hidden purpose underneath it all.

"Oh, Mother, Father, look!" Victoria's elated voice drew his attention to the railing where the young lady pointed. "You can see the lighthouse from here."

"Lighthouse? Where?" Jacob strained his neck to see over the rail.

Matthew came alongside and gave him a boost with his knee. "Right over there. See where Victoria is pointing?"

As if Matthew had asked the question of him and not Jacob, William's eyes followed the invisible line that extended from Victoria's finger and stopped at the impressive structure standing tall and high above the ground. He'd only been nine when the lighthouse had been built, and he'd begged Father to take him to the unveiling. Recently he'd learned there were plans for the building of a newer lighthouse made out of marble, but it seemed the actual construction was still a few years away.

A few minutes later, the ferry docked and the passengers disembarked. William waited for Annabelle's family and then his to step off before him. For some reason, he felt like remaining at the back of the assemblage. It often ended up being his position anyway. Why change things?

They all walked along the main paved road that looped around the park, opposite the typical flow of carriages. About one hundred feet into their stroll, Annabelle glanced over her shoulder and gave him a questioning look. He mustered a smile for her. It must have worked. She returned the smile and a moment later resumed her original position.

When she wasn't preaching at him, Annabelle actually had many appealing qualities. He'd never forget the squeal when Jacob held that hornworm up to her face. The interest she had shown in baseball at the game and her thoughtful gesture in getting those tickets still impressed him. Her infectious enthusiasm was contagious. Just a few minutes in her presence and William found himself relaxing or even once in a while forgetting about his problems.

That spelled danger. Her sparkling blue eyes, beautiful smile, melodic laughter, and unassuming behavior made him want to do nothing more than remain in her presence as long as possible. Every time she appeared, though, it became harder and harder to maintain his seeming disinterest.

"Mother, do you think we might picnic near Muskoday Lake today?" Annabelle tucked her hand around her mother's arm and leaned close. "We always go to Tacoma Lake, but Muskoday was just formed last year. I'd love to enjoy the island from a different perspective."

"I don't mind if your father doesn't," Mrs. Lawson replied. "Brandt, dear? Shall we alter our standing plans and try something new this afternoon?"

Mr. Lawson shrugged. "As long as the Berringers are all right with that, I have no objections."

"We are fine with wherever you would like to settle," William's father answered on behalf of his family.

With their new destination decided, they stopped and changed direction toward the east instead of the west. They'd be farther away from the lone wooden bridge and casino, but they'd have a much closer view of the lighthouse.

Annabelle fairly bounced at her request being accepted. The ruffles of her skirt swayed to the left and right as she walked and drew William's attention. She seemed so carefree and full of life. And why not? She didn't have to work a farm plot or share living space with eight other families. That brought him back to the folly of thinking about her as anything but a friend.

After all, what did he have to offer her?

William scuffed his shoe on the gravel beneath his feet and kicked a few tiny rocks out in front of him. He couldn't take her on carriage rides or invite her for an afternoon stroll through the park. Today was the closest he and Annabelle would come to what life might have been like had his family not lost everything—and they were surrounded by both of their families.

He knew she was interested, but his present station made him hesitate. It wasn't that he didn't want to pursue something with her. On the contrary, he didn't feel comfortable just yet. Being a lady, she'd never initiate anything with him. So he was right back where he'd started—wondering and chastising himself for even thinking of her in that way.

"Well, here we are!" Mrs. Lawson announced.

William had been so lost in thought that he hadn't even noticed they were close to the new lake. Three large blankets were unfolded and spread out on the ground. A minute or two later, the two large picnic baskets Mr. Lawson and William's father had been carrying were set down and opened.

Jacob stood at the edge of one of the blankets. "I want to go see the horses and the stables and take a pony ride."

How had his brother heard about the riding stables? They'd only been constructed earlier that year.

"Victoria told me about them when we were on the ferry," Jacob added as if he'd heard William's unspoken question.

"After you eat some lunch, dear," his mother stated.

"But I'm not hungry."

"Jacob." His father's tone brooked no argument, and Jacob knew it. The frown he made and the way he crossed his arms said he didn't like it, but he'd obey.

William almost laughed. There were times he forgot just how much of a boy his brother was. He worked hard on their piece of farmland and seemed so grown-up at times. Today, though, he was all boy.

As the two families shared the delicious meal of roasted chicken, coleslaw, potato salad, and almond-glazed sponge cake the Lawson's cook had prepared, conversation flowed on a number of different topics. William knew he should try to keep up with them and offer some input, but between the sermon that morning and being here with Annabelle and her family, he couldn't. There was so much circling in his head—he needed to make sense of it all. The sooner he finished, the sooner he could excuse himself and take a walk. Maybe that would help clear his thoughts.

After tossing the final bone on his plate, he wiped his mouth and hands and stood. Everyone looked up at him, and his parents shared a joint curious expression. He'd better make this quick so they could all return to their socializing.

"Mr. and Mrs. Lawson, you must extend my compliments to your cook. The meal was quite tasty. But if you'll excuse me"—he allowed his gaze to roam over each person in turn—"I believe I'll take a walk and enjoy this fresh air."

Jacob immediately jumped up, almost upsetting his plate, and looked at his parents. "Does that mean we can go see the horses now?"

"And maybe the verandas on the outside of the casino, too?" Victoria looked to her own parents, a hopeful yet pleading look on her face.

Great. If the other adults agreed, he'd likely end up being asked to escort them. So much for his solitary walk. He really needed some time alone to sort out a few things.

"I'd be happy to go with them," Matthew offered. "That is, if Mr. and Mrs. Berringer approve."

That was something William didn't expect. He might be free of the others after all. And that meant he could still take his walk.

Both sets of parents did agree. In what seemed like seconds, plates were abandoned and the threesome headed toward the road. Maybe he should ask Annabelle if she'd like to join him. Then again, that would defeat the intention of being alone.

"I believe I'll join them all as well."

So much for that idea.

Annabelle wiped her mouth and gracefully stood. After

.

stepping around behind her parents, she caught his eye.

He tried to read her expression, but he could only decipher a confusing mixture of disappointment and acceptance. As she walked by him to join Jacob and her brother and sister, William had second thoughts. Should he have invited her anyway? What about their parents all watching and listening? That would have started them talking for sure.

Avoiding the temptation to see if anyone still paid him any mind, he took off toward the outer loop. The rest of them had chosen Central Avenue as a more direct path to where they were headed, but he preferred to circle Lake Okonoka and walk by the pier on the south side of the island.

William had no idea how much time had passed when all of a sudden he found himself at the eastern edge of Tacoma Lake. The casino Victoria had mentioned earlier wasn't too much farther. If William kept walking, he might run into the four of them.

Instead, he found a shady spot under a big oak and settled on the grass, staring through the trees to where he could just make out the roof of the casino. Even though he hadn't been there in two years, he could still see it in his mind's eye.

The two-story Queen Anne-style building with its corner towers and covered exterior walkways was a popular meeting place for many on the island. Its gabled wood structure had even been where William's cousin had gotten married two years ago. The residents of Detroit had begged the city to turn Belle Isle into a public park emulating the tree-lined boulevards of Paris. Following in the pattern established by Frederick Olmsted, this meetinghouse for social events added just the right touch.

"Would you mind some company?"

William startled at Annabelle's hesitant voice behind his left shoulder. She sounded and appeared rather nervous. He hastened to his feet and faced her.

She held her hands clasped together with fingers hooked. "Forgive me if I interrupted your solitude. I was just walking around the perimeter of Tacoma Lake when I saw you. But I can continue on my way if you'd rather be alone."

"No, please." He almost spoke without thinking and said that was exactly what he wanted—for her to leave him in peace. One look at her face, though, and all thoughts of dismissing her flew from his mind. He extended his arm toward the space he'd unofficially claimed. "Sit."

After gathering her skirts in her hand, she settled on the ground and assumed a most ladylike perch, legs tucked underneath and to the left. He wished he had a jacket he could have laid down for her so she wouldn't have to soil her pretty blue dress. It set off her eyes perfectly. He joined her on the ground and couldn't take his eyes off her. If anyone happened by, they'd just assume the two of them were courting. For the first time since they met, William wished they were.

Silence fell between them. He wanted to say something, but his tongue was tied in knots and his brain refused to register any coherent thought beyond how pretty she looked.

"Amazing to think that a man who also designed Central Park in New York came up with the plans for Belle Isle as well. Don't you agree? Did you know this island actually belonged to Chippewa and Ottawa tribes and they named it Wahnabezee, or Swan Island, to start?"

William released a sigh. At least she managed to come up with something to start the conversation again.

"It was owned by the French and then British before American settlers finally claimed it. Then the city of Detroit bought it just fifteen years ago and named it Belle Isle."

Her voice trembled a bit. Could she be as nervous as he was right now? If so, maybe things weren't as hopeless as he'd thought. There was only one way to find out.

He cleared his throat. "Yes, and I much prefer Belle Isle to Hog Island, like the French had named it."

Annabelle covered her mouth and giggled. Turning her head to look at him, she lowered her hand and smiled, a twinkle making her blue eyes shine. "I would have to agree with you there. Naming a beautiful island such as this after a pig doesn't exactly seem like the proper choice."

The tension seemed to be broken. Laughter almost always had a way of helping.

Extending his long legs out in front of him, William leaned on his hands. "You mentioned the designer when you first approached. Frederick Olmsted. Did you also know he resigned before any of his designs for this island were actually begun?"

Her eyes widened. "No, I didn't. What happened?"

"The city had already approved everything, so they went ahead with his plans anyway."

Annabelle looked out over the lake. He followed her gaze as she shifted it to the north where the tree-lined path offered shelter to numerous couples out enjoying the day.

"I'm glad they did," she said a moment later. "I can't imagine this island as anything other than what it is. My family has been coming here for years."

"It reminds me a lot of Mackinac Island," he said without thinking.

Her head swung toward him once more, and surprise spread across her face. "You've been to Mackinac?"

Oh no. He hadn't intended to let something like that slip. Then again, why not? She knew his family hadn't always been living the way they were now. What harm could come of sharing a little from life prior to the current state of affairs?

Shifting to lean back on his elbows, William crossed his legs at his ankles and stared straight ahead. "Yes. In fact, we used to go at least once every year near the end of the summer. Just two years ago, we were at the hotel to witness a demonstration by an agent of Edison Phonograph of their new invention."

"On the front porch? I've been there to see that, too!"

He glanced over to see her close her eyes and draw her hands up to her chin.

A sigh slipped from her lips. "It's the most beautiful hotel I've ever seen. The tulips, daffodils, and geraniums all create such vivid color."

For a fleeting moment, William wondered if they might have been on the island at the same time. Perhaps they even stayed at the hotel during the same week. No, that wasn't possible. He would have remembered someone like Annabelle.

"My parents were actually married in a gazebo on the island before the hotel was built." She opened her eyes and tilted her head toward him with a soft grin on her lips. "And it was on that island where they both realized neither of them had been honest about who they really were."

William drew his eyebrows together. "What do you mean?"

She placed her hands in her lap. The grin turned into a full-fledged smile. "Oh, it's one of my favorite stories to tell." Shifting so she faced him, she continued. "When they met, they both were pretending to be someone they weren't. Mother took a job at a candle factory to achieve some independence and assist a woman who was part of her charity work. Father assumed the position of a simple refinery worker to appease his own father before achieving a management position there."

That seemed logical enough. "So how does Mackinac Island factor into everything?"

"Well," she began, flattening her hands on her lap, "at the

end of the summer the year they met, their families both traveled to the island. And unbeknownst to them, their parents had already met behind their backs to plan their meeting. Their entire pretense came to a halt the first night they were both there."

William could imagine what type of meeting it must have been. If they had been lying to each other all that time only to learn they both belonged to elite families, it must have been a miracle they ended up together. Something didn't quite make sense, though.

"If they found out they were both from upstanding families, then wouldn't they be happy?"

"Well, that's just it," Annabelle replied. "Mother thought Father was nothing more than a refinery worker, and her parents had already cautioned her against pursuing a relationship with him. And Father had a similar edict issued from his father regarding Mother. My uncle Charles had already caused a bit of a scandal with a young woman not of his class. Grandfather Lawson didn't want to see a repeat of that."

William nodded, starting to understand. "Ah, so despite their attraction, neither one of them thought they could do anything about it."

"Exactly. And when they came face-to-face on the island, dressed in formal attire, well, you can probably imagine the result."

He could imagine it, all right. Only he wasn't thinking about her parents' meeting. All he heard was the clash that resulted between two families when they believed their status in society didn't match. If even a hint of that remained with Annabelle's parents, he didn't stand a chance.

"I never have agreed with all the conflict, though," she said, interrupting the negative turn his thoughts had started to take. "I mean, if two people care about each other, where they live or who their families are shouldn't matter." She pinned him with a direct gaze. "What do you think?"

Her question caught him off guard. "I. . .uh. . .uh. . ."

For the life of him, he couldn't come up with a logical response. What *could* he say to that? Trying to break the hold her gaze had on him so he could compose himself, he found it impossible. Her eyes seemed to be saying something he didn't dare hope to assume. Could this be her way of saying she considered him more than a friend? Or was he simply imagining it?

William didn't want to read more into the situation than actually existed, yet he had to fight not to reach across and take one of her hands in his. He could throw caution to the wind and tell her he agreed. Or he could take the safer route.

"I think it should be up to the two people involved." Yes, the safe path was best. . .for now. "They should be honest with each other first and take it from there."

"Oh," she replied, her voice containing a hint of disappointment.

Had she wanted him to say more? To get more personal, perhaps? He wanted to, but would she accept what he had to say? William opened his mouth to test the waters, but another familiar voice interrupted before he could begin.

"There they are! Come on, Jacob. Hurry, Matthew."

Victoria. William sighed. He looked toward the northern side of the lake to see his brother running behind Annabelle's sister with Matthew bringing up the rear. Annabelle also shifted her attention to the trio approaching.

No sense trying to continue their conversation now. Hopping to his feet, he stood and turned to extend a hand down to Annabelle. She looked up at him and hesitated. A second later, she placed her soft hand in his and allowed him to help her to her feet. The change in position brought her just inches away from him.

As she lifted her chin, her mouth parted, drawing his eyes to the charming pink of her lips. Shoving that idea to the back of his mind, William again found her eyes and searched them for a sign—any sign at all. She didn't waver in her gaze, and that was when he saw the spark.

"Oh, Annabelle," Victoria called, interrupting the moment. "You missed seeing the geese and the swans. They were so beautiful."

The spell was broken, and Annabelle turned to face her sister, pulling her hand free from him. William took a step back and tried to get involved in the ensuing conversation. His mind refused to cooperate, though. Annabelle felt something for him. That much he knew. He just didn't know what or how much.

Still, even a little made a difference. And that helped him sort out his feelings somewhat. Maybe God had a greater plan in all this after all. Maybe his circumstances weren't as bleak as he thought. Only time would tell.

twelve

Annabelle couldn't help the smile that formed on her lips. "Have you heard the news?"

William stood in front of her and held out his plate at the last station in the food line. She normally worked closer to the center. Today she hoped it would work to her advantage.

"What news?" William asked, his eyes appearing to pick up on her enthusiasm.

"About the Pullman strike."

It had been two weeks since their afternoon on Belle Isle, but her work had kept her too busy to follow up on their conversation since that day. Perhaps today would be better.

She placed a rather large slice of berry pie on his plate. It was hard to believe he wasn't aware of the outcome of the strike. Even with his limited exposure out here in the fields, he always seemed to have extensive knowledge about current events.

Two lines formed on his brow as he drew his eyebrows closer together. "No, I haven't. Has there been another development?"

Annabelle looked at the next person in line. She'd love more than anything to stand and talk with him, but other workers needed to be served. With a quick glance behind her then back at William, she made an attempt at nonverbal communication.

It took a second or two, but understanding dawned on his face, and he nodded. "Pardon me," he said to the worker waiting next to him. "I'll be out of your way in just a moment."

William stepped to the end of the table and selected a patch of dirt about five feet away. Annabelle served pie to the worker in front of her.

"Enjoy," she said with a smile as he took his plate and left.

William crossed his legs like an Indian and settled his plate on his knees. It hadn't been all that difficult to persuade him to stay and talk. He could have just taken his meal and left. Obviously she hadn't imagined his interest that afternoon on the island. As he took his first bite, she continued to serve.

"So tell me," he said after swallowing a bite of beef. "What is this splendid news you have to share about the strike?"

She glanced from the corner of her eye but maintained her focus on the workers. "Well, you know the results of the strike during this recession and how it affected transportation west of Chicago."

"Mmm-hmm," he replied as he took another bite.

"Mr. Debs and the American Railway Union have tried hard to sustain their momentum."

"Yes, and they even resorted to violence in order to achieve their goal. At least supporters did," he added.

She'd read the horrific reports of some of the tactics used. The obstruction of tracks and walking off the job was one thing, but attacking those who broke the strike and setting fire to buildings was quite another. Those who continued to work were only looking out for their own interests. They didn't deserve to be treated cruelly for that.

"I don't understand how the loss of life would help aid their cause. If anything, I'd think it would cause more complications."

"Well, sometimes people don't always think before they act." He took a long gulp of water. "Sometimes their ultimate goal makes them blind to the pain they might cause by acting on their passions."

"I wish they could somehow achieve their goals without all the violence."

"That's how we eventually end up with wars."

"This is true." Annabelle sighed. Only in a perfect world would violence cease to exist. As long as men were left to their own devices, hostility and bloodshed were sure to be the end result.

"You were going to tell me about the recent news."

"Oh my! You're absolutely right." How could she have gotten so off track?

William chuckled and speared a forkful of vegetables. "It's all right. But if you don't share this exciting report, I might be forced to seek my information elsewhere."

Annabelle turned her head to catch sight of the grin William tossed her way and the teasing gleam in his brown eyes.

"Very well." She pursed her lips. "Now, where did I leave off?" She honestly couldn't recall.

"I believe you had mentioned something about the strike workers doing what they could to maintain their momentum."

"Ah yes. Two days ago, I overheard Father and Mother talking. It seems the strike has now collapsed, and the plant has reopened."

"What about the workers who went on strike?"

"I believe Father said they're now in jail. Something about ignoring an injunction that forced them to cease their activities or risk being fired."

His eyebrows rose. "Injunction? That means the company must have managed to secure counsel on their behalf."

Leave it to William to understand the procedures and have a better grasp on the details than she. Annabelle tried hard to remember what Father had said. Perhaps she could impress him with that.

"Yes, and President Cleveland actually stepped in to send

in the army and a U.S. marshal, saying something about the strike interfering with the delivery of the United States mail."

"Oh, you know, I hadn't thought about that." William rubbed his fingers over his chin. "But I can see how that would be the case." He grinned. "I mean, you can't stop the mail service. That alone should be a federal offense," he said with a wink over the rim of his cup as he took a drink.

Annabelle planted one fist on her hip. "You're teasing again, aren't you?"

He laughed. "Yes, Miss Lawson, I am. But that doesn't take anything away from the fact that you have paid excellent attention to the developments of late and provided sound information." Then he sobered and nodded toward the other side of the table.

She turned back around, pleased. Her memory hadn't failed her, and William was indeed impressed.

"Can I have two pieces?" asked the young lad in front of her. He couldn't be more than twelve or thirteen, and that meant he had a healthy appetite, too.

"Of course." Annabelle served the boy and glanced down at the thinning line. Only a few more minutes and they'd start the cleanup process. There was more than enough pie left. Maybe she'd even save a second piece for William as well.

"You know, you have just the right disposition for something like this."

His remark took her by surprise. Was that a compliment?

"What do you mean?"

"The way you respond to the workers and those who make special requests," he explained. "You return the right amount of kindness and generosity that keeps folks coming back for more."

She fought hard not to look at him or react in any significant manner. He certainly had made a sudden about-face regarding his treatment of her. If she had to pinpoint the moment it happened, she'd never succeed.

"And you're persistent, too," he added. "Especially with folks who can be a bit stubborn."

Annabelle had to strain to hear that last part. He spoke it under his breath, and from the way he ducked his chin to look at the ground, she had no doubt he was referring to himself.

"Mother would say I come by it honestly," she replied in an attempt to put him at ease. "Father would say it's all part of my charm."

"I might be inclined to agree."

She started to respond, but he didn't give her a chance.

"This pie is delicious." He held up his fork with a rather large piece of pie sitting atop it, but he didn't quite meet her eyes.

Annabelle couldn't tell if he was attempting to cover up the remark he made about her charm or if he didn't consider the remark anything out of the ordinary. She didn't have much experience with men. Today she wished she did. Being able to interpret hidden meanings might make this conversation easier.

She heard the scrape of fork on plate and looked down to see that he'd just finished the pie.

"Would you like another piece?" She pointed at the table then reached for one of the two pies remaining, holding it up for him to see. "There is plenty here. And I certainly don't intend to consume the leftovers."

William paused as his gaze traveled from her face to her feet and up again. Her cheeks warmed at his open admiration and perusal. In fact, if she didn't miss her guess, he actually approved.

"Mr. Berringer?"

Her father's voice startled her. How long had he been

standing there? Not long enough to have witnessed William's bold and obvious assessment of her appearance, she prayed.

William presented the picture of calm control as he stood and set his empty plate on the table next to Annabelle then shifted his attention to Mr. Lawson.

"Yes, sir?"

"Could you tell me where your father is? I'd like to speak with him for a few moments."

"Um, I believe he and my mother are eating with Jacob over at our plot."

"Excellent. Thank you." Father nodded then turned toward her.

She held her breath, wondering what he might say and praying it wouldn't be asking her to leave her place to help Mother.

"Annabelle, you did a fine job today. I know the workers," he said with a quick glance at William, "appreciate your dedication."

Exhaling, she relaxed a little. He could have said a lot more, especially where William was concerned. Annabelle said a silent prayer of thanks that he hadn't.

As Father stepped away toward the main fields, he again gave her a pointed look. "Will you be ready to accompany me home when I return?"

Only clearing and wiping down the tables remained. "Yes, I should be."

"Very good. Then I shall make a point to stop here before leaving."

She and William both watched her father head away from them. No doubt about it. Father had observed the exchange between William and her prior to announcing his presence. He didn't have to come out and say it. She could tell. And if she didn't miss her guess, there would be a conversation about it later.

"Well, I didn't expect to see your father here. Do you know the topic of that conversation?"

Annabelle hoped it wasn't a direct result of what Father might have witnessed between William and her. On the contrary, she prayed it was because Father had found a lead or two in the business world for Mr. Berringer.

"I'm not certain," she said truthfully. "He did seem rather intent on finding your father, though."

"Miss Lawson," William began, pivoting to face her. "Do allow me to apologize for anything I might have said or done that could be improper."

He obviously had seen the same thing she had from her father. Why else would he be asking for her forgiveness? *Had* he done anything wrong? She didn't think so.

"There is no need for a confession or defense of your actions, Mr. Berringer," she said softly. "But if it helps ease your mind, your apology is accepted."

"Thank you." He visibly relaxed.

Annabelle understood his trepidation. Her father could be a rather intimidating man when he wanted to be. It only endeared William to her more to see how much he respected her father and how eager he was to clear his conscience or make certain he was held in high esteem in her eyes.

"Now," he said, smacking his hands together. "How can I help?"

⁂

The soft murmur of voices traveled into the front hallway as Annabelle made her way toward the sitting room. Just as she'd predicted, Father wanted to speak with her. During the carriage ride home from the potato patches, he'd asked her to join him for a meeting before dinner. He made it clear Mother would be present as well.

Whatever they had to say, she prayed it wouldn't be something she didn't want to hear. But first she had to face her parents. There were a lot of possibilities, and only one way to find out.

Before she stepped into view, she took a deep breath and willed her heart to settle down to a more even pace.

"Ah good," Mother announced as soon as Annabelle walked into the room. "Please, dear, come take a seat and join us."

Well, she didn't sound upset. That had to be a good sign. In fact, she actually sounded quite pleased.

Annabelle's feet sunk into the woven carpet as she headed straight for her favorite settee. By all appearances, her parents were giving her no reason to be concerned. Each of them sat in wingback chairs opposite her and presented the image of relaxation. Father leaned back in the chair and rested his hands on the arms. Mother tucked her legs underneath her with her hands folded in her lap. When neither of them said anything, Annabelle swallowed and wet her lips.

Finally, Father spoke.

"Before we get to the primary reason for asking to speak with you, your mother and I want to make it clear that we are more than pleased with the work you've done at the fields."

"Yes," Mother added. "In fact, your selfless acts of service have gone far to ensure the continual high spirits of the workers."

"Compared to reports from other plots, the productivity levels from that area of the city have even caught the attention of the mayor."

Annabelle didn't know how to respond. They made it clear that complimenting her wasn't the purpose of this conversation. She appreciated the fact that they made it a point to begin with that, though. Still, anticipating what might come next made her heart race again. If that didn't give away her nervousness, her erratic breathing would.

Father again resumed control. "Now, for the matter at hand."

A matter? Annabelle shifted her legs to cross her left ankle over her right. She slowly smoothed her hands on the folds of her skirt. It helped absorb the dampness of her palms as she awaited Father's next words.

"Annabelle, you know your mother and I only want the best for you. But before we present several opportunities to you, there is something we must know."

First there was a matter. Now they had a question about that matter. Then they had an opportunity for her? Just where were her parents heading with all this?

Father leaned forward and clasped his hands together, resting his forearms on his knees. "You came to me a few weeks ago asking that I make a few inquiries on behalf of the Berringer family. As a result, we suggested you invite them to join us for a picnic on Belle Isle."

Ah, so that invitation had been extended for more than mere socializing. They were looking to learn more about the Berringer family. Well, at least the day had been a good one—even if her parents had ulterior motives.

"But it has come to our attention that a good portion of your time is spent in the company of the eldest Berringer son."

Annabelle shouldn't be too surprised to see the focus on William. The thought *had* crossed her mind earlier near the end of lunch. She just didn't think it would be treated in such a serious manner. They hadn't done anything untoward.

"With that in mind," Father continued, "we'd appreciate your honesty in answering the following question."

She knew what was coming, but she wasn't sure she could provide an answer that would satisfy her parents.

"What are your feelings regarding William Berringer?"

Annabelle opened her mouth to speak, but no words came out. She swallowed twice and tried to gather her thoughts. Considering William more than a friend had only been a viable option as of their visit to Belle Isle. Now her parents expected her to make sense of her feelings and put them into words?

"Annabelle, dear," Mother interjected, breaking the silence. She narrowed her eyes and peered into her daughter's face. "Do you simply not know how you feel?"

Clearing her throat, Annabelle tried again. "Father, Mother, I must confess. Up until today, Mr. Berringer and I had been nothing more than friends. Other than attending the baseball game, nearly every one of our conversations has centered around his anger for what had happened to his family or where he stood in his faith."

"And now?" Father pressed.

"Now?" She wet her lips again. "Now I don't know. I admit that I'm attracted. Any more than that, I don't believe I can say for certain."

There. She might not have given them the response they sought, but she had been honest.

Several moments passed as Father and Mother exchanged silent communication with each other. Father angled his body toward Mother and raised his eyebrows. Mother nodded in response. Annabelle sat in silence, awaiting what felt like a sentencing, even if she knew that was a rather substantial exaggeration.

Finally, Father returned to his original position. "It's clear to us that you have been nothing less than honest, and for that we are grateful." His expression brightened then, and he again sat back in his seat. "Now that we have that settled, we're faced with the issue of your social activities with eligible men."

Her heart fell, and her shoulders dropped. She should have known this conversation would present itself again. And on the heels of asking her about William, it made perfect sense. Her parents wanted her to pursue other relationships.

Mother sat up straighter, eagerness replacing the previous

concern. "We have been speaking with several of our friends and believe we've found several young men we'd like you to meet. Each one of them is quite poised to assume solid positions either in their father's footsteps or in a venture they've begun on their own."

She wished she could muster up a bit more excitement in response to this announcement. Although she couldn't say for certain where she and William stood, she wasn't eager to pursue a relationship or possible romantic entanglement with someone new. Nevertheless, her parents had gone to all the trouble on her behalf. As their daughter, she owed them her respect and cooperation. And that's exactly what she'd give.

"Is there anything you'd like to say in response?"

Annabelle took a deep breath. "Well, I must confess that this comes as a surprise today. I have no doubt that you do have my best interests at heart," she added with a soft smile. Best to do what she could to set them at ease. "I am, after all, eighteen."

"A fact that hasn't been lost on us, I assure you," Father said, his voice a mixture of remorse and pride.

"Be that as it may, I'm well aware that my friends are all married or engaged or headed in that direction. I'm just grateful you were more patient than other parents regarding any arrangements."

"We're well aware of what can come of wanting to force certain outcomes," Mother replied. "As you know, your father and I endured that very thing not long ago. We agreed that we didn't want to do the same to you."

"I appreciate that, Mother. But I suppose it's time for me to take the matter of my relationships a bit more seriously." She looked at them both before continuing. "You've both given me so much. How could I not honor your wishes?"

Maybe with this shift in her priorities, she could continue to explore possibilities with William as well.

"However," Father stated, "where Mr. Berringer is concerned, we must caution you."

What? Just when she thought her parents were providing the perfect opportunity for her to answer all the questions floating in her mind regarding William, Father throws this into the mix?

"But, Father, it isn't like that at all." She unclasped her hands and extended them in a placating gesture. "I already said he is only a friend." At the moment that much was true in reality. Her thoughts, however, were another matter. "Are you saying that I can no longer spend any time with him or his family?"

Father pressed his lips into a thin line. "What I'm saying is that prolonged interactions with him on a social level might prevent you from seeing certain possibilities with the other gentlemen you meet. I've done what I can in regard to possible job opportunities for both him and his father. Anything further is up to them."

He hadn't set William apart from the class of a gentleman. That had to be something.

"But how will I avoid spending time with him when his family works at the very area where I volunteer all my time?"

Annabelle knew very well what the answer might be. She prayed the actual one would be different.

Father hesitated, and she could tell what he was about to say wasn't easy for him. "Then I suppose we have no choice but to limit the time you spend volunteering." Father inhaled and released his breath in a loud sigh. "For the time being, let's say only once a week."

Mother nodded and pursed her lips. "I do not see any cause to end your charity work completely, Annabelle, dear. But I agree with your father. William might be respectful and possess exceptional manners, and we know he's simply fallen on difficult times, but until he can reestablish himself, anything beyond friendship is not wise. At least not at the moment. There are more than enough young men right here who I'm sure will provide a suitable distraction."

She didn't come right out and say it, but Annabelle could read between the lines. It wasn't that William might distract her from the other men. It was his current status as a farm worker, not a member of their elite society. After what her parents endured in their own lives, she'd have thought they'd be more lenient. At least they didn't forbid any association at all with him. They were only limiting her. That left her with no choice but to abide by their wishes—no matter how much it pained her.

"Thank you, Mother. Father." She regarded them each in turn and dipped her head in acknowledgment, maintaining a polite exterior. "I admit I will miss the time I am giving up, but I promise to devote appropriate attention to the potential suitors I might meet as well."

Her parents both stood, seeming pleased with the outcome and Annabelle's promise.

"That is all we ask, dear," Mother said.

"Now let's adjourn to the dining room where I'm sure Katie has an appetizing meal ready."

Annabelle allowed her parents to precede her from the sitting room. That conversation hadn't gone as she'd have liked. It could have been much worse, though. At least she was still permitted to continue her volunteer work. Of course, once a week didn't leave opportunity for much. If anything more was to happen with William, God would have to work a miracle. She had to trust Him and leave it at that.

thirteen

William brushed his hands over the tops of the tomato plants as he moved from those rows into the potatoes. He might not be the best farmer, but any man would be proud to walk among the results of their months of hard work.

Movement to his right caught his attention, and he looked up to see Annabelle crossing the field toward him. He started to smile and call out to her. Then he noticed her demeanor. She didn't look anything like the same vibrant young woman he'd seen only a week ago. With slumped shoulders and head down, this Annabelle was like a completely different person.

"Good afternoon, Miss Lawson," he greeted in an attempt to ease whatever might be bothering her.

The way she dragged her feet and the fact that she had yet to make eye contact with him said a lot. What could have possibly happened to cause such a drastic change? She hadn't responded, so he tried again.

"Is something the matter?"

This got her attention. Slowly she raised her eyes to look at him. A frown marred her pretty face, and her eyes had lost all their shine.

"Mr. Berringer," she began in a hesitant voice, "I've come today to let you know that you'll only be seeing me once a week from now on."

"Once a week? Is everything all right?" He'd gotten rather used to seeing her several times a week. Knowing that would no longer be the case interrupted the sense of calm he'd begun to have where she was concerned.

"Well, to be honest, no. At least not to me."

"What happened?"

The sigh she released was full of regret. "Remember when Father came last week?"

"Yes."

How could he forget? When his own father had told him about the meeting and shared they might have found an open door or two, he'd been thrilled. That Mr. Lawson would go to all that trouble on their behalf meant a lot to him. His father had seemed impressed as well. How could anything following that meeting cause Annabelle to be so unhappy?

"Later that afternoon, just before dinner, my parents invited me into our sitting room to speak with me. And the result of that conversation was to tell me two things."

She lowered her eyes again. He had a hard time believing the ground held much fascination, so he waited and gave her time to say what she'd come to say.

"The first was to inform me they had several young men they'd like me to meet."

Oh no. Parents arranging meetings for their daughters with eligible men usually meant one thing. They were intent on finding a good match and would likely encourage a short engagement period once one was found.

"The second was to say that my volunteer time here would be limited to once a week."

At least they hadn't forbidden her entirely. They would just have to make the most of the time they did have. It didn't seem as hopeless as she made it seem. He opened his mouth to respond, but she held up a hand and raised her gaze to his. The sheen of tears took him by surprise.

She sniffed. "That means the time we spend together will likely be during the noon meal I'll be serving and nothing more."

By her reaction, he could tell she didn't like what her parents had to say. Yet, as a dutiful daughter, she could do nothing less than obey. A sense of honor like that wasn't easy to find these days.

"Did they give a reason for this abrupt change?" William had his own ideas, but he wanted to hear Annabelle say it.

"Only that spending more time with you might hinder me from seeing the merits in the other gentlemen they wish me to meet."

Well, those weren't exactly the words he assumed Mr. Lawson had used, but the meaning was the same. He might have gone the extra mile to speak with his associates and done so out of the goodness of his heart, but that didn't change how the man obviously viewed him and his father.

"I tried to reassure them they had no reason to worry about our friendship. But they were convinced that restricting my time here would benefit everyone involved."

Sure it would. William stared beyond her to the expansive fields. If they prevented her from spending time with him and limited even the time they *were* together to supervised areas, it would be quite difficult for them to share any private moments. By enforcing this edict, everything would go according to her parents' well-thought-out plan. Eliminate the possible competition—him. He had to admit, they seemed to have thought of everything. And they appeared to have noticed the attraction even before he had a chance to speak of it with Annabelle or hear her respond in kind.

"Do you not have anything to say, William?"

The sound of his first name coming from her lips shook him from his thoughts. Had she even realized what she'd said? He returned his gaze to her face, only to find a silent pleading in her eyes combined with a lone tear that slipped down her cheek. If he had any doubts about her feelings before, he didn't have any now.

"I'm afraid I don't know what to say, Miss Lawson."

He almost used her first name as well. Only if he did that,

he might forget himself. Or worse, he might fool his mind into believing that something more between them already existed. He wished it did, but neither of them had spoken of it yet. No, maintaining his distance was the best option at this point.

"It's clear how your father feels about me." He sighed. If only things were different. "And to prove that I'm unsuitable, he's not only forbidden you from spending unsupervised time with me, but he's also cut back the frequency of your visits."

"He hasn't completely ruled out all my visits, though," she retorted with hope in her voice. "I'm still able to come here once a week."

"Yes." He looked down and kicked at the dirt beneath his feet. "Once a week. That seems more like a charitable allowance on their part so they can say they didn't put an end to your work entirely."

William hadn't intended to take out his frustration on Annabelle. She didn't deserve to be the recipient of the misplaced irritation directed at her father, especially when he was more upset with himself for not doing something sooner. And she didn't deserve to have what little hope she still held dashed by his doomsday frame of mind. He couldn't seem to stop himself, though.

"Miss Lawson, I believe it's best if we see the current turn of events for what it is." He risked a glance at her and forced his expression to remain unaffected—at least where her tears and pleading were concerned. "A sign from God that our friendship will have to remain just that. A friendship. Nothing more. Your parents have made sure of that."

She flinched with his final words. Her lower lip trembled, and it tore at his heart. He refused to put her in a position, though, that might require her to defy her parents. There was only one way to ensure that.

"Miss Lawson, we should both accept things the way they

are and make do." Letting her down like this wasn't what he wanted to do, but it was for the best. If he didn't put an end to this now, he might rethink his decision and confess his feelings. "Now, if you'll excuse me, I have work I must do."

"But—"

William didn't give her a chance to respond. Instead, he kicked the dirt again then removed his cap and slapped it against his thigh. A part of him wanted to turn around to see if she would follow him or leave. But if he did that, he'd lose all resolve. He did have things to do, and he couldn't allow her sentiments or emotions to interfere. Otherwise he might not succeed.

&

One week later, Annabelle made her dutiful appearance at the potato patches to serve the noonday meal. She did her best to offer a smile to each worker. Kind words or conversation of any kind beyond a simple "You're welcome" or "Have a nice day" were out of the question. Her heart simply wasn't in it.

Last week when William had stormed off and left her standing there alone, she thought she'd crumple in a heap right then and there. She had hoped he might protest with more force or, better yet, tell her he wanted more than friendship and ask her how she felt. What he said and did, though, had caught her off guard, leaving her with no response. Instead, she'd returned home dejected and asked her mother to move forward with the introductions to her first gentleman of choice.

She might not be able to be with William, but at least she could conceal her hurt and pain behind the guise of social engagements and the pretense of getting to know the men her parents insisted on parading in front of her. If she played her role well, no one would be the wiser.

Not even the excitement of hearing the state fair would

once again take place in Detroit could penetrate her self-inflicted despondency. Whenever anyone spoke of it, she remained silent, nodding where appropriate and displaying a smile she didn't feel.

She hadn't counted on facing Mrs. Berringer or Jacob again, though. It made sense. They did have to eat, after all. She just figured they might skip this week. Well, hoped anyway. It looked as if that wouldn't be the case today. Only this time, Mr. Berringer and William were notably absent. She glanced farther down the line to see if they just might have arrived late. No, they weren't there, either. Was William avoiding her? If so, why was his father gone as well?

"Afternoon, Miss Annabelle." The little boy greeted her with a smile as wide as could be.

One look at his face, complete with the customary dirt marks and unkempt hair falling in his eyes, and she nearly lost all control.

"Hello, Jacob," she managed through the thickness in her throat.

"I'm extra hungry today, so give me lots and lots."

In spite of herself, she smiled. Even so, she didn't feel it. "Very well, Jacob. You'd better eat it all, though. I don't want to see you throwing any of it away."

"Oh, you won't," he said, licking his lips. "I promise."

"I have a feeling he means what he says, Miss Lawson," Mrs. Berringer added. "So you had better take him at his word."

Annabelle did as he asked then turned to his mother. "The normal amount for you, I assume?"

Mrs. Berringer tilted her head and regarded her for a few moments. "Yes," she finally answered, sounding distracted. "Tell me, dear, is everything all right?"

"Everything is fine, Mrs. Berringer," she lied, averting her eyes. Perhaps Jacob and his mother would take their meals and leave her be.

"Somehow I have a feeling that's not entirely true, Miss Lawson." Mrs. Berringer reached across the table and placed a hand on Annabelle's arm. "Come find me when you're through here." She started to usher her son farther down the line then paused and pinned Annabelle with a meaningful look. "Please," she added.

Annabelle wanted to make her excuses and say she had to clean up afterward and might not have the time. However, the words wouldn't come. Instead, she nodded, touched by the tenderness she saw in the woman's eyes. Perhaps Mrs. Berringer would have some answers to her dilemma.

෴

About an hour later, Annabelle swiped her cloth across the table and stacked the last pot in the wagon headed back to the collection center. Her heart pounded as she made her way around the tent where most of the other remaining workers were. If she took care, she could slip away without her mother noticing. She just wasn't ready to answer any questions about her destination.

Besides, her parents hadn't said she couldn't talk to the Berringers at all. They simply cautioned her regarding William. And he wasn't even here today.

Placing two fists at the small of her back to work out a few kinks from all the bending and scrubbing, Annabelle made her way across the field to the Berringers' land. Mrs. Berringer hadn't said she'd be there, but it was the most logical place to look first. As she approached, she caught sight of a lone figure walking slowly up and down the rows and inspecting the various plants. For a moment Annabelle had thoughts of those little worms she'd seen William and Jacob plucking from the leaves. At least Jacob wasn't here to provide a repeat performance.

As she observed Mrs. Berringer further, she noticed the

woman appeared to be saying something. Or perhaps she was singing to herself. No—there was no sound coming out of her mouth. Then Annabelle realized what it was. Mrs. Berringer was praying. Annabelle almost didn't want to intrude, so she stopped.

Mrs. Berringer looked up when she was still fifteen feet away. It was almost as if she'd been expecting her right at that moment. A welcoming smile broke out on the woman's lips.

"Miss Lawson, I'm glad you decided to come. I was beginning to wonder if I needed to come find *you*."

Now that certainly would have caused a scene. Mother would have been sure to see Mrs. Berringer and ask a lot of questions. She intended to speak with her mother very soon but not today. All things considered, Annabelle was glad she came here.

"Why don't you join me on the blanket I have set out there, and let's have ourselves a little chat."

Annabelle peered over Mrs. Berringer's shoulder to see the coarse horse blanket laid out on the ground. The woman obviously had this all planned out. A dented and worn teakettle in desperate need of a polish sat on one corner of the blanket with two tin cups next to it. She'd thought of everything it seemed.

Again words failed her, so she nodded and followed Mrs. Berringer's lead. Zipping a quick prayer heavenward, she petitioned God to give her the strength to get through this conversation without completely breaking down.

Lucille dipped her hands in a small bucket of water set off to the side then dried them on her apron. "Feel free to do the same if you wish. Although I'm sure you had ample opportunity to do that back at the food tent."

"Yes," Annabelle replied. "But thank you just the same."

Mrs. Berringer tilted her head to the side and pursed her lips. "You have a lot of weight on your mind. I can tell.

Something troubles you, does it not?"

William's mother was nothing if not direct. Now she knew where Jacob got it. For a moment Annabelle thought about making up something different to tell Lucille. But one look at the kindness and wisdom she saw in the woman's eyes disarmed her. Perhaps if she shared her heart with Mrs. Berringer first, she'd be better prepared when she spoke with her own mother. Maybe it would help her sort out a few things in her mind.

"Yes, as a matter of fact, it does. Am I correct in assuming that's tea in there?" She nodded at the kettle.

"Yes," Mrs. Berringer replied, reaching for one of the cups. "Would you like some?"

"If you don't mind, I'd love some."

"But of course, my dear. I prepared it just for you." She poured and handed Annabelle the cup. "So you see, it's a good thing you did come. Otherwise I might have been forced to either drink everything in this kettle or dump it out. And I do so hate to waste anything if I can avoid it."

How long had it been since she'd sat with her mother like this, talking about anything and everything? A few months at least. And that was too long. A pang of guilt struck her that she wasn't confiding in her mother. She'd do that at the earliest opportunity. For now she'd make the most of this situation.

William's mother settled in place and gave Annabelle her undivided attention. Her motherly demeanor reached out and touched Annabelle's desperate longing to share her innermost struggles.

"Drink your tea and tell me what's on your mind. . .or perhaps your heart."

Yes. No doubt about it. Lucille was straight to the point, just like Mother. The build up of concerns that burdened Annabelle's weary soul teetered right on the edge of her lips, wanting to spill forth like water from an upended pail. Her thoughts scattered in every direction at once.

"I. . .I'm not sure. I mean, I don't know," she babbled, trying to gather her thoughts into some semblance of coherency. "I hardly know where to begin."

"Maybe I could help somewhat?" the kindly woman asked.

"Please," Annabelle encouraged.

"I am quite certain a good bit of what is plaguing you is somehow connected to my son. If I'm not correct, stop me now."

Annabelle dipped her chin and whispered. "No, you're correct."

"And if I haven't missed my guess, it's because you have feelings for my son yet are torn because your parents have limited your time here at the fields."

Annabelle could hardly believe it. All those emotions tumbling around inside her wanting release, and William's mother had summed it up in just a few words. Sometimes hearing it spoken from someone not involved in the mess proved beneficial. Meeting Mrs. Berringer's gaze over the rim of her teacup, Annabelle blinked back the tears that had gathered.

"I can see the purpose behind Mother and Father doing what they did. I mean, they are only looking out for me, keeping what they believe are my best interests at heart." She shook her head and wiped away the overspill from her cheek with the back of her hand. "And I truly believe that of them," she declared. "I just don't agree with how they're going about it."

"Have you spoken with them about this and told them how you feel?"

"No. Not yet."

"Then I strongly encourage you to be honest. It's clear your parents love you, but how can they truly know what's best if you don't share the truth in your heart?"

Mrs. Berringer was right. She had told them only what she knew they'd wanted to hear, so her current situation was as much her fault as theirs. "You're right. They had asked

for my input, but I didn't refute anything. And William"—
Annabelle sighed, remembering their last conversation—"he
didn't even allow for a rebuttal of any kind from me. He just
reacted and walked away."

Instead of acting surprised, Mrs. Berringer simply nodded. She no doubt knew her son quite well, and this behavior
wasn't unexpected.

"Unfortunately, William gets his impatience and impul-
siveness from his father. But he means well, even when he
doesn't show it."

"Yes, I know that. The last time I saw him, I could tell he
was fighting a battle all his own," Annabelle said hesitantly.

"I will confess," Mrs. Berringer began, "William did
come to see me after he spoke to you that day. He confessed
everything he was feeling and even shared about your sad-
ness, but he knew that moment was not the right time
to do anything about it. I could tell that hurt him a great
deal." The regret in her tone spoke volumes. "He always
wants to fix things, to come up with solutions. Feeling like
his hands are tied is not a good place for him to be, nor a
comfortable one."

William? Hurt by her sorrow and what she had said that
day? She thought back. There had been a definite melancholic quality in his mannerisms. And if she called it what
it was, she had seen the hurt his mother now mentioned.
He'd covered it so quickly, though, she hadn't been sure at
the time. Then he'd stormed off and was now nowhere to be
found, leaving her to interpret his true feelings.

"I'm so sorry, Mrs. Berringer. I would never intentionally
hurt William. But he deserved to know what my parents had
dictated."

"He cares a great deal for you, you know."

Care for her? After the way she'd initially shoved all those
Bible verses at him instead of waiting to get to know him

better? Then again, there was the afternoon on Belle Isle and the teasing moments they'd shared at various times. Still, hearing it from his mother felt odd. She had wanted to hear it from William first.

"You must be mistaken."

Lucille squared her shoulders. "I know my son, Miss Lawson."

Now she'd done it. Annabelle should know better than to imply to a mother that she was wrong about one of her children. "Please forgive me, Mrs. Berringer. I didn't mean to imply that you don't, but William hasn't exactly given me a lot of substantial evidence to prove that statement. There have been moments when it's seemed clear, but I'm still not sure."

William's mother placed a warm and comforting hand on Annabelle's arm. "He tries to hide it, but a mother knows the heart of her son." She took a final drink of her tea and smiled. "Give it a few days. And trust God. I have a feeling everything isn't quite as hopeless as it might seem right now."

Annabelle continued to ponder those words long after she left and returned home. As she'd confessed to Mrs. Berringer, there had been times when William appeared to feel the same as she, but he'd never spoken the words aloud. Besides, how could he possibly care about her if he was intentionally avoiding her?

What was a girl to think? She sighed. As Mrs. Berringer had said, there was little left to do but wait on the Lord. If no one else knew what was on William's mind, He would. Now she had just one thing to do. Wait. All right—two things. She had to speak with her Mother.

❧

Felicity reached out and wiped a tear from Annabelle's cheek and smiled. They sat facing each other in the two wingback chairs in the study, their knees almost touching.

"Why didn't you speak of this sooner? The conversation your father and I had with you would have been the perfect time."

Annabelle offered a rueful grin. The confession had gone a lot smoother than she thought it might. Thanks to the brief preparation during her earlier chat with Mrs. Berringer, she had been able to share her heart with Mother with more clarity.

"I am sorry I didn't say anything then, Mother. But I thought you and Father had already made up your minds. And I suppose since I myself didn't know where William stood, I didn't feel comfortable at the time." Even now the explanation sounded weak. In truth, she didn't have a good reason for holding back.

"I could tell something wasn't quite right that day," Mother said with her keen understanding. "When you didn't protest at all, though, I assumed you were being forthright as usual. I'm glad you've decided to be honest this evening."

Remorse filled Annabelle. She should have told Mother how she felt from the start. She'd made foolish decisions in the past, and this would be added to that list. "I know. And my reasons don't even make sense now." It felt like a great weight had been lifted from her shoulders. "I'm so relieved I didn't allow this to go on any longer."

Mother clasped one of Annabelle's hands in her own, giving her a loving squeeze. "As am I. We have always been able to talk about anything. I don't like it when I feel there's an unexplainable rift."

"Nor do I." Annabelle sighed. "But where does that leave us now?"

Mother pressed her lips together in what appeared to be an apologetic expression. "Well, I cannot cancel on some of the meetings that have already been put in place, but I promise not to arrange any further ones." Amusement danced across her face. "I only ask that you at least give these young gentlemen a chance."

"I shall remain cordial at all times." Annabelle giggled. "Unless, of course, one of them becomes insufferable."

"Your father and I have chosen these men quite well. I highly doubt you will encounter a circumstance such as that." A twinkle entered Mother's eyes. "But if you do, I give you full permission to put an early end to the outing."

It felt so good to relate like this again. The past few months hadn't been a good measure for the depth or closeness she shared with Mother. Now things had been put right again, and they could move forward from here.

All she needed now was to hear William admit his feelings himself. She prayed it would happen soon.

fourteen

Everything seemed to be falling into place. One of the open doors turned into an opportunity beyond his wildest dreams. All because Mr. Lawson had taken the time to make a few inquiries. William could hardly wait to find Annabelle and tell her the good news. He should probably thank Mr. Lawson as well, but he wanted to start with Annabelle.

Of course, she'd have to agree to see him first. With the way he'd left things the last time they spoke, he might have ruined his chance of that.

Only one way to find out.

"Berringer, do you have a moment?"

William paused on his way out the door of the Edison factory and turned to see the man who would soon become his supervisor.

"Sure, Mr. Hudson. Something on your mind?"

Ralph Hudson came to stand before him, a serious look in his eyes and his mouth formed into a thin line. Had William done something wrong already? He hadn't even started working yet. That couldn't be possible. Could it?

Hudson motioned to a bench near the main walk to the building. "Shall we sit?"

This sure felt important. At least half a dozen possible scenarios ran through William's mind.

"Mr. Berringer, first allow me to reassure you this has nothing to do with our interview earlier this morning."

William released a silent sigh. All right, so that answered one question.

"But there was something I gathered from your response

when I remarked about the kindness of Mr. Lawson in informing us of your name in the first place." Hudson put up one hand in a staying motion. "I could be way off base, and if I am, I invite you to correct me."

With a shift of his arm from the back of the bench to his lap, William wasn't sure if he should respond or wait for Mr. Hudson to continue. William was thankful the man decided for him.

"I know the Lawson family rather well through our various business dealings. Although this recent financial recession has left us not keeping in touch as much as we once did, I know Mr. Lawson to be a rather devout Christian, putting his love for God above everything else. Your acquaintance with Brandt made me speak with Mr. Edison on your behalf." Hudson kept his gaze direct and steady. "When I remarked that God had brought you to our company, your disposition changed. Do you perhaps not agree?"

That was the last thing he expected Mr. Hudson to ask. "Pa—pardon me, sir?"

"I assure you that your response to my question bears no weight whatsoever on my decision to hire you as my assistant. This is strictly for my own benefit."

William looked down at his lap then stared out across the street. So it wasn't something he had done; rather, it was his reaction. Returning his gaze to Mr. Hudson, he took his time in formulating a response. After all, God and His plan had been the very thing that had plagued him for weeks—ever since hearing that sermon the Sunday they went to Belle Isle. In fact, a lot had happened that day.

"Sir, I will not disagree with your assessment of Mr. Lawson's character and devotion. In fact, his entire family follows his lead. I have no doubt it's what caused his daughter to speak to her father on my behalf in the first place."

"His daughter?" Hudson quirked an eyebrow. "Annabelle?"

A slight grin formed on the man's lips as he nodded. "So that's the real connection, then. I had wondered how Lawson managed to find you."

"Yes, sir. Miss Lawson has spent a great deal of time helping the workers on the land where my family farms." William brought her beautiful face to mind, an easy feat considering how often he'd thought of her lately. "She has given so selflessly, while at the same time making no attempt to hide the fact that her faith in God is what led her to get involved."

"Was that the reason, then, for the change I mentioned?"

"That was part of it."

William wasn't sure how much he should share. He didn't know Hudson at all. Then again, the man had taken the time to seek him out to speak on matters related to God. Perhaps it was God's way of saying He was indeed still looking out for him.

"As you are no doubt aware, Miss Lawson can be rather persuasive when she sets her mind to something."

Hudson chuckled and rested farther against the bench, draping one arm across the back. "Well, I don't know her as well as I know her father, but from what I hear, yes. That is true."

"And I'll confess, sir, that when my family suffered so greatly following the failed banks, I blamed God."

"That's understandable."

"When Miss Lawson arrived and seemed to make me her target for her personal crusading, it only angered me further."

Hudson seemed to follow his thought process. "And now?"

"Now?" William appreciated Hudson's desire to get to the point. "Well, sir, how could I not see God's hand in everything that's happened lately? I never fully turned my back on Him. I was just angry." He thought of how persistent Annabelle had been and how often evidence of God's involvement had almost smacked him in the face. "I highly doubt this all happened by chance."

"You are right about that. And don't misunderstand me. Your qualifications are the reason you were hired. However, hearing what you've confessed, I see it was God at the center of it all."

William offered a slightly nervous chuckle. "Guess I have some thanks to be giving."

"Perhaps to a certain young lady as well?" Hudson suggested with wisdom and an acute perception in his eyes.

A lazy grin formed on William's lips at the idea of resuming his original plan to go find Annabelle. "Yes. I believe that's in the works as well."

Hudson stood, and William did the same. The man extended his hand, which William took. "Mr. Berringer, I look forward to having you join us on our team. This company is poised right on the edge of some amazing developments. I don't know about you, but I'm looking forward to being a part of these exciting times."

"As am I, sir." William dropped his hand. "Now if you'll excuse me, I do believe there is someone I must seek out."

Hudson held up both his arms in surrender. "By all means, my boy. Don't let me delay you any further."

As William walked away, Hudson called to him.

"We'll see you first thing Monday morning."

Monday. After the past year and a half of struggling, it almost seemed impossible that his life was about to change in such a profound way. Yet it would. For that, and so much more, he owed God, Mr. Lawson, and Annabelle his gratitude.

❧

William paused just outside the door to Mr. Lawson's study. The butler had directed him down the hall and said Mr. Lawson was expecting him. Of course he was. William had requested this meeting. Now that he was here, though, his stomach clenched and tension rippled across his shoulders.

With a quick prayer for strength, he took a deep breath and raised his hand to deliver two short knocks to the closed door.

"Come in!" came the immediate response.

He turned the knob and pushed the door open, stepping into the darkened interior and immediately removing his hat. His eyes searched the room and found Mr. Lawson standing next to his desk. The man's expression was too difficult to read from this distance, though.

"Mr. Lawson," William plunged forward. "Thank you for seeing me on such short notice."

"It's my pleasure, Mr. Berringer."

Annabelle's father didn't make any attempt to move from where he stood, so William approached him instead.

"I know you probably have a lot of business to attend to, so I won't take up too much of your time. I just wanted to come here today to thank you in person for all you've done on behalf of my father and me. You're no doubt aware that we have both secured positions at Edison Illuminating Company, and for that we owe you a great deal of thanks."

"I'm pleased to hear everything has worked out. And I was happy to do what I could to help."

The man William thought might be intimidating was anything but as his congenial expression became clear. Whatever preconceived notion he'd formed in his mind about Annabelle's father that might paint him in a less than appealing picture vanished. In its place was a man William looked forward to getting to know better. If things went the way he hoped, he'd have ample opportunity in which to do so.

"Father and I both begin work Monday. In fact, I have just come from the meeting where the job was offered to me. I didn't want to wait any longer before letting you know how much I appreciate your interventions."

"I'm glad you did come, son. It says a lot about you and affirms so much of what my daughter has said when she's spoken of you and your family."

William licked his lips and shifted from one foot to the other, turning his hat in his hands. Mr. Lawson's approval meant so much, but standing before the man still put him on edge.

"I won't deny the fact that I've been aware of her feelings for you for quite some time now. And I won't make you any more uncomfortable than you are by asking your intentions toward my daughter. I am certain they are honorable."

"Yes, sir."

Mr. Lawson nodded. "Very well. We'll leave the rest for another time." The hint of a grin tugged at the corners of the man's mouth. "I have a feeling a more personal conversation with my daughter at the center of it will be forthcoming before too long."

Annabelle's father was astute. William had to give him that. He swallowed and nodded, unable to speak beyond the tightness in his throat.

"Now if you'll excuse me, I do have some rather important matters that require my attention before supper." He winked. "And I don't want to upset Mrs. Lawson by being late."

"No, sir!" William grinned, grateful he'd again found his voice.

"I trust you don't mind seeing yourself out?"

"Not at all, sir." William turned toward the door then glanced over his shoulder. "Thank you again, Mr. Lawson."

"You're quite welcome."

❧

All right. That was it. Annabelle had just ended her outing with her most recent suitor—and her last. As Mother had requested, she'd seen these engagements through to fruition. Now she was glad to put an end to them. None of the men she'd met held any appeal, nor did she see them anywhere in her future.

On the contrary, the only man she consistently saw in that future hadn't been around for several weeks. That didn't mean he hadn't been far from her thoughts. In fact, with each new social event, William became more and more a forerunner in her mind. With this last outing, she had even imagined William's face across from her instead of the man who escorted her.

Being patient was getting her nowhere. Annabelle had promised her parents to go to the potato patches only once a week. But she couldn't avoid it any longer.

She had to find William.

As Annabelle marched across the adjoining plots, resolute and focused, her tunnel vision prevented her from seeing anyone or anything around her. Before she realized it, her trek had brought her to the Berringer land and straight into the solid form of William Berringer.

"Umph!"

William immediately placed his hands at her waist and saved her from a fall. She looked up into the amused eyes of the very man she'd come to see. After all this time and how easily it seemed he had made himself scarce every time she came to the fields, Annabelle thought she'd have plenty to say. Unfortunately, her tongue refused to cooperate.

"Mr. Berringer!" was all she managed to get out.

"Tell me, Miss Lawson, do you often make it a practice of not looking where you're going?"

His eyes crinkled with laughter, and the brown in them lightened as his lips quirked into a grin. Her heart raced at the appealing image he presented. Then she remembered all the pain of the weeks of separation. He might have been helping her abide by her parents' wishes, but to her, he'd abandoned her. Plain and simple.

She took a step back, forcing him to drop his arms, and planted both fists on her hips and frowned. "Well, under normal circumstances, no. However, you've been absent every other time I've ventured onto your land in the past few weeks." She shrugged, doing her best to remain unaffected by his nearness. "I didn't expect to run into anyone."

William winced as her words hit their intended mark. Annabelle didn't truly desire to hurt, but even she felt the sting delivered by her response. Still, he needed to know.

He sighed, and his shoulders drooped. The mirth in his eyes dimmed as well. "Miss Lawson, I do apologize for my behavior since we last spoke. Please believe me when I say that you have not been far from my thoughts, despite how we parted."

She almost admitted the same thing. Instead, she held her tongue and waited for him to continue.

"There really is no excuse for my deplorable actions, and I was actually planning to come find you today so I might tell you so." He implored her with true penitence in his eyes. "I also came to ask for your forgiveness in the hopes that we might repair whatever rift I might have caused."

Well, that confession certainly took the wind out of her sails. How could she deny a request like that? In spite of herself, the hurt and pain she'd been feeling at what she'd viewed as his desertion vanished. His sincerity reached deep and touched her heart. Her puffed-up desire for some form of vindication deflated, leaving behind the soft spot she'd reserved only for him.

"Mr. Berringer, I appreciate your honesty. Your apology is accepted." She nearly smiled at how he visibly relaxed. "Might I ask for your forgiveness as well?"

Confusion wrinkled his brow. "My forgiveness? For what?"

"I harbored some resentment after you stormed off that day, and prior to that, I hadn't been the best example of patience regarding your anger at God or your slip in faith."

"About that," he began. William licked his lips and swallowed twice then offered a sheepish grin. "I've finally been able to make peace with everything and realize that God indeed has been looking out for me and my family all along."

Annabelle gasped. That confession seemed to come out of nowhere. It was the last thing she would have expected to hear from him today. Yet she could see in his boyish demeanor and the expression in his eyes that he meant every word.

"But how. . .I don't under—" She paused to gather her thoughts, unable to keep the surprise from her voice. "What happened to bring about this change?"

Almost instantly a wide smile transformed his face. It reached all the way to his eyes. An answering smile started to form on her lips as hope made her catch her breath.

"That's the other reason I wanted to come find you. I've got a job!"

Heedless of propriety, Annabelle jumped forward and threw her arms around William's neck. A second later, his arms came around her waist. He swung her once in a circle as his laughter sounded in her right ear.

"Oh, William, that's wonderful!" she spoke over his shoulder. Then realizing where they stood and what she'd just done, she released her hold and put a little distance between them, tucking her chin against her chest. "I'm sorry."

He chuckled. "Don't be. I didn't mind."

Annabelle looked up to see that his eyes had darkened. He now regarded her with an emotion she didn't dare name. Not when it bordered so close to what she wanted to show as well.

"So tell me," she began, attempting to return her pounding heartbeat to normal. "What is this job, and when do you begin?"

"It's for Edison Illuminating Company, and I started three weeks ago as the assistant to one of the supervisors. You might even know him. Mr. Ralph Hudson."

"Oh my! Yes. At least I know who he is. Father is more familiar with him than I. But I have met him on more than one occasion." She drew her eyebrows together. "He's rather important with the Edison Company, is he not?"

William nodded. "From what I gather. What's even more amazing is the fact that my father has been offered a position as a financial consultant for the company. So not only do I have a job, but he does, too." He reached for her hands, holding them lightly in his own. "So you see? With the abundance of good fortune, God and I had ourselves a little chat." He grinned. "I hadn't exactly been fair in my anger at Him. Tossing aside years of faith because of present circumstances doesn't say much of me. It took the wisdom of another believer, my parents' steadfast faith, and the admittance of my own stupidity to get me back on track. Now God and I are back where we used to be."

Annabelle gave his hands a slight squeeze. "You have no idea how glad I am to hear that, Mr. Berringer."

"What's with the formality? A moment ago you used my first name."

She had? Perhaps the hug they'd shared blotted that out. "Oh," she muttered, lowering her eyes.

William dropped one of her hands to touch her chin and raise her gaze to his once more. "As I said, there is no need for apologies. I liked it. And I'd like it if you did it from now on."

"I don't believe that would be proper," she protested. Then again, this would be a step in the right direction if what she thought might come next truly did.

"On the contrary, I must disagree. After all the time we've shared and the conversations we've had, I would say it's entirely proper." His eyes regarded her, mirth again dancing in his brown depths. "Would it help if I said please?"

A giggle escaped from her lips at how adorable he looked.

"Very well."

His voice lowered and became quite gentle. "Very well, what?"

"Very well. . .William," she whispered.

"There, now that wasn't so difficult, was it, Annabelle?"

Hearing her name coming from him sounded so nice. She could see why he preferred it.

"All right, now that we've got that out of the way, there's only one more issue to address."

"What's that?"

"Gathering our families to celebrate the recent good fortune and share in the gratitude my father and I owe your father."

"That sounds like a splendid idea!" Annabelle already knew Mother would agree. With a little persuasion, she was sure Father would, too.

"I've already thanked your father privately, but—"

"You have?" When had he done that? And why hadn't Father told her about it?

"Yes. I believe a dinner would be the best way to commemorate everything."

He made it sound so uncomplicated, speaking of meeting with her father and now moving forward with plans to gather their families together again.

"It sounds as if you've given this a great deal of thought."

"I have. In so many ways." He squeezed her hands. "And before we discuss the details of the dinner, there is another matter I wish to discuss. No—make that confess."

Annabelle's breath hitched. Was he about to say what she'd been hoping he'd say for a while now?

"I haven't been all that great at sharing what I've felt." William grimaced and released a nervous chuckle. "Unless of course it was my anger at God." He held her gaze with his own and licked his lips. "Despite my boorish behavior, you never gave up and in the process became quite important to me."

Annabelle bit her lower lip, trying hard to contain her excitement.

"So before I make a mess of everything, I'm going to come right out and say it." He inhaled once. "I care a great deal for you and need to know if you feel the same."

"Yes!" she immediately replied, fighting the urge to embrace the man in front of her again.

William saved her the effort by pulling her to him instead. "That's the best word I've heard all day," he said, wrapping his arms around her back.

She nestled against him. It would be so easy to stay there forever. But she remembered how she hadn't told anyone she'd even come here today.

"Oh no!"

William stared at her with a quizzical expression in his eyes and eyebrows drawn. "That wasn't exactly what I expected to hear next. Annabelle, what's wrong?"

"I shouldn't be here today. Mother and Father are sure to wonder where I've gone."

"Oh, is that all?" He visibly relaxed and grinned. "Then let's make sure you get home safely, shall we?" He maintained his hold on her left hand and turned. "We don't want to jeopardize anything we've accomplished to this point, do we?"

William winked, and a blush warmed her cheeks. They hadn't yet made any promises, but at least their feelings were out in the open. Beyond that, they'd discover it together. For now Annabelle basked in the joy of Willam's returned affection. Anything else was mere icing on the cake.

fifteen

"Are you sure everything is in place?"

Annabelle peered at the break in the curtain then glanced back at William, worry etched across her face.

"Relax, Annabelle." William stepped away from the table where he'd been setting up a few items loaned to him courtesy of the Edison Company. "You have worked hard with that handful of women from the Ladies Aid and managed to accomplish quite a lot in a short amount of time."

"I know." She inhaled a deep breath. "But there is so much about this evening that must go right."

He walked up behind Annabelle and turned her gently to face him. Taking her hands in his, he gazed down into her blue eyes. "Everything will go just fine. Do what you told me many times to do not so long ago."

"Trust God," they said in unison.

She smiled. "I do. I'm still nervous, though."

William raised one hand to trail a finger down her soft cheek. "So am I. However, this is all going to work out just fine. It *is* the State Fair, after all. We didn't have one last year, and it hasn't been here in Detroit for eleven years. That's bound to make everything better." He implored her with his eyes. "Even if there are any glitches."

"I pray you're right," she replied, the tremble in her voice belying her lingering doubts.

He leaned forward and placed a kiss on her forehead. "I am. Trust me." Tapping her nose with his finger, he grinned. "Why don't you head on over to the stage area so you can be sure your parents make their way here without delay?"

She nodded. "All right. We'll be back shortly."

After she left, he returned to see to the final details.

He and Annabelle had indeed worked hard the past two weeks. They never would have made it happen without the help of his newly formed connections at the Edison Company. Not to mention his own parents. When they learned of his plan and the promise of seeing Annabelle more often, they'd eagerly agreed to help.

With everyone working together as a team, they had secured the private area now cloaked in the thick, tentlike curtain on all four sides. The candelabras on the tables in the center cast a soft glow, and the place settings had been transported from one of the finer restaurants in Detroit. Even now the tantalizing aroma of the dishes prepared for this meal reached his nose and made his stomach rumble in response.

William cast an analytical look around the makeshift room, a sense of pride filling him at all they'd achieved. He sent a silent prayer of thanks to God, along with a request that His hand remain on all that would be taking place in a matter of moments.

All he needed to do now was make sure his special guest was in position.

❧

"Annabelle, where are you taking us?" Mother demanded.

"I must admit, your cryptic invitation on behalf of young Mr. Berringer has piqued my interest," Father added. "But I also hope it involves food. I'm famished."

Annabelle grinned. She did her best to hide it from her parents, though. The more secretive she could be, the better. The less they knew, the better the surprise would be.

"You will both be quite pleased, I assure you," she promised.

The rest of the trek took place in silence. As they reached

the entrance to the curtained room, she prayed for peace. If only her heart would return to its normal position instead of lodging in her throat. It made breathing rather difficult.

At that very moment, the curtain parted and a maid dressed in black with a white apron stepped outside.

"Mr. and Mrs. Lawson. Miss Lawson," the young girl greeted. "Please come in."

The gasps from both of her parents as soon as they entered filled Annabelle with pride. She caught sight of William standing at the opposite side. His wink sent her heart racing.

"Oh! It's all so beautiful," Mother gushed.

"I *am* impressed." Father inhaled an appreciative breath through his nose. "And if the meal tastes half as good as it smells, I will say you and Mr. Berringer have outdone yourselves."

"Yes." Mother looked all around the room. "But the question still remains. What is all this about?"

"If you will take your seats, Mother and Father, you will find out in just a few moments."

As soon as they sat, William opened the curtain where he stood and ushered in his parents along with Jacob, followed by Mr. Hudson and his wife. Matthew and Victoria brought up the rear. Annabelle smiled at her brother and sister, who moved with the entourage to gather at the table, each one sitting where his or her name card indicated.

William walked to the head of the table and cleared his throat. All eyes turned toward him, waiting expectantly.

"First, I want to thank all of you for agreeing to come this evening." He caught Annabelle's eyes for a brief second. "Miss Lawson and I appreciate your presence. We both agreed to begin with the purpose of this evening."

Annabelle took her eyes off William long enough to look at Father, who regarded William with obvious pleasure. Mother smiled as well.

"Now," William continued. "If you will indulge me a moment longer, I need to preface our remaining guest by way of an introduction."

He had originally suggested they wait to bring in their guest of honor until after the first or second course, but Annabelle had pleaded with him to start the dinner by introducing him. She would never make it through her first bite otherwise. And it would only add to the enjoyment of the evening.

Everyone looked to the two chairs that still remained empty, one where William stood and the other immediately to the right, next to where Annabelle sat. William pinned his gaze on Father. His throat muscles moved as he swallowed several times, and his hands gripped the back of the chair in front of him hard enough to make his knuckles turn white.

"Mr. Lawson. You and I already spoke about this that day in your study, but I felt a celebratory dinner would better demonstrate the full scale of my appreciation and that of my family for all you've done to help us. And as you surmised that day, the other topic has indeed become an issue."

William relaxed his grip on the chair and inhaled a deep breath. Annabelle did the same, sharing his apprehension. There was no going back now.

"Sir, I am well aware of how much you love your daughter. I also know that considering my former state of affairs, I was not deemed an acceptable suitor."

Father didn't show any surprise at hearing that word, and Mother grimaced. They shared a private look between them that spoke volumes. Chagrin fleeted across both their faces, and Annabelle was glad to see they regretted discounting William simply because of his current status.

William forged ahead. "However, as I said that day, my intentions are completely honorable, and I would not dare to make this request if I didn't feel you would even consider it a possibility." Another deep breath preceded the final rush of words. "You see, I have come to care a great deal for your daughter. Now that I am settled into my new position, I feel the time is right to pursue a further relationship with her. With your permission of course," he hastened to add.

Ripples of delight rumbled through those gathered. Mother and Father remained stoic, but Annabelle caught the sheen of tears beginning in Mother's eyes. Mr. Hudson sat back in his chair, a measure of satisfaction reflected on his face. The others made no attempt to hide their reactions.

"Before you respond, though, and without further ado"— William raised his voice and turned toward the opening where he'd at first been—"I'd like to invite our remaining guest to now join us."

The curtain parted, and in stepped Thomas Edison. As he approached the table, Father, Mr. Berringer, Matthew, and Mr. Hudson all stood.

Annabelle had never met the gentleman, so she took the time to observe his appearance. Dressed in a tailored suit and a bit older than she'd expected, Mr. Edison's receding hairline was parted on the side and brushed over. He carried an air of importance about him and commanded immediate attention.

Mr. Edison immediately approached Father. "Mr. Lawson," he greeted as they shook hands.

"Mr. Edison." Father nodded. "It is good to see you again."

Annabelle couldn't remain silent a moment longer. "Do you mean you know each other?"

"Yes, as a matter of fact, we do." Father acknowledged Annabelle then returned his attention to Mr. Edison. "Although it has been some time."

Mr. Edison agreed. "When Mr. Hudson extended the invitation for me to join you all this evening, care of Mr. Berringer, I was delighted to accept. Am I to understand this charming young woman and one of my newest employees are responsible for this evening?"

Pride reflected in Father's face at Mr. Edison's favorable remark. "Yes, I do believe that is correct."

"Well then, my compliments to you both." Mr. Edison dipped his head with a smile at Annabelle then turned to face William. "Mr. Berringer, allow me to say to you directly that I am happy to have you working at my company and look forward to the benefits you and your father both will bring to the team."

"Thank you, sir."

Father cleared his throat. The attention then shifted to him as he prepared to speak. "And before we are all again seated to begin partaking of a meal that promises to be just as memorable as this evening already is, I would like to say a few things."

He stepped around his chair and moved to stand next to Annabelle. With a slight motion of his hand, he beckoned William to approach.

"Mr. Berringer, I would be remiss if I didn't acknowledge all the hard work you and my daughter have put into making this evening rather special. And I would also be quite the fool if I denied your request from a moment ago." He lightly clasped Annabelle's chin in his hand and bestowed a loving smile upon her before again directing his gaze at William. "You have more than proven yourself as a worthy suitor. I am impressed with your tenacity and unwillingness to give up on something you obviously wanted so much." Extending his hand toward William, who accepted it, Father continued. "It's clear to me that you two make an excellent team. You may continue with my blessing."

Annabelle's heart soared at the final pronouncement. Joy filled her to the core. "Oh, Father, thank you!" She placed a kiss on his cheek and threw her arms around him in a quick embrace. Relaxing her hold, her eyes drifted to William, whose face reflected the satisfaction she also felt at their attempts resulting in success.

Father again stepped back to allow them to move closer together. Mindful of all the other watchful eyes, Annabelle simply bestowed a kiss on William's cheek before leaning against him as he wrapped one arm around her waist and pulled her to him.

"Mr. Lawson," William began. "I am grateful for the trust you've given me." He glanced down at Annabelle with a smile. "And the treasure. I promise to treat both with the utmost care and attention."

Father wagged a finger in William's direction. "See that you do, my boy. I'll be keeping my eye on you."

William chuckled. "I wouldn't expect anything less, sir."

Mr. Edison moved to his place at the head of the table, again drawing everyone's attention his way. "Now that that's settled, let's eat, shall we?"

Hearty exclamations of agreement sounded. A blur of frenzied activity accompanied the verbal responses. Annabelle stood within the protective and warm circle of William's arm, watching their friends and family.

It all felt surreal. She had fully expected Father to protest a bit more, or for some other hitch to happen in their plans. But nothing did. It flowed so well, there was no doubt God was at the center of everything. All of her worrying and fretting seemed like such a waste of time and energy. As William had said, she should've trusted. Ironic that he would have to remind her when she was the one to help bring him back to his faith.

"Looks like everything has worked itself out. I have your father's blessing, a good job, and a promising future." He tightened his hold. "And best of all, I get to share it with you."

Annabelle turned and looked up into William's eyes. His smile was reserved only for her. "Who would have thought that such a blessing would have come out of such adversity?"

"Yes." William stepped back and drew Annabelle with him until they were a few feet from the table. "I spent so much time being angry, and God still brought you into my life in spite of it. I don't deserve you, but I sure am glad you're here."

She giggled. "Me, too." Annabelle wrapped her arms around his waist and grinned, "I know I chose the best."

He chuckled and drew her closer. "And the best is what you're going to get. I promise. Just make sure you remind me to trust God when times get tough again."

"I will." She cast a look over her shoulder at the table. Everyone seemed to be oblivious to their absence, but that didn't mean they shouldn't participate.

William nodded toward the others. "Do you think anyone would miss us if we took our plates and ate in private somewhere else?"

Annabelle jerked her attention back to him to see if he was joking or not. The twinkle in his eyes gave her the answer. "I believe they would. But perhaps we can enjoy our dessert alone later."

Casting a quick look to the left and the right, William touched his forehead to hers, a crooked grin appearing on his lips. "That sounds like the perfect end to the evening."

"Now, will you join me, Mr. Berringer?" She held out her hand, palm down, in his direction.

He took it and tucked her arm into the crook of his elbow and bowed. "Yes, Miss Lawson. I do believe I will."

A Letter To Our Readers

Dear Reader:
In order that we might better contribute to your reading enjoyment, we would appreciate your taking a few minutes to respond to the following questions. We welcome your comments and read each form and letter we receive. When completed, please return to the following:

Fiction Editor
Heartsong Presents
PO Box 719
Uhrichsville, Ohio 44683

1. Did you enjoy reading *Hearts and Harvest* by Amber Stockton?
   ❑ Very much! I would like to see more books by this author!
   ❑ Moderately. I would have enjoyed it more if

   _____

   _____

   _____

2. Are you a member of **Heartsong Presents**? ❑ Yes ❑ No
   If no, where did you purchase this book? _____

   _____

3. How would you rate, on a scale from 1 (poor) to 5 (superior), the cover design? _____

4. On a scale from 1 (poor) to 10 (superior), please rate the following elements.

   ____ Heroine   ____ Plot
   ____ Hero   ____ Inspirational theme
   ____ Setting   ____ Secondary characters

5. These characters were special because? _____

_____

_____

6. How has this book inspired your life? _____

_____

_____

7. What settings would you like to see covered in future
   Heartsong Presents books? _____

_____

_____

8. What are some inspirational themes you would like to see
   treated in future books? _____

_____

_____

9. Would you be interested in reading other **Heartsong
   Presents** titles? ❏ Yes   ❏ No

10. Please check your age range:
    ❏ Under 18   ❏ 18-24
    ❏ 25-34   ❏ 35-45
    ❏ 46-55   ❏ Over 55

Name_____

Occupation _____

Address_____

City, State, Zip_____

PRAIRIE HEARTS

Three women of the 1890s dream of romantic adventure, but can they possibly find it in the small town of Cedar Bend, Kansas? When Carrie Butler's runaway buggy is stopped by a handsome drifter, she believes her dreams have come true. But John Thornton has come to dig up old secrets in town. Mariah Casey has found purpose in mothering an orphan, but romance eludes her until she meets a handsome rancher. But when Mariah clashes with Sherman Butler's daughter, romance may escape her again. Joanna Brady's prayers for excitement seem to be answered in the appearance of a dangerous wrangler. But Clay Shepherd is not the marrying type.

Historical, paperback, 352 pages, 5⅜" x 8"

HEARTSONG

PRESENTS

If you love Christian romance...

$10.99

You'll love Heartsong Presents' inspiring and faith-filled romances by today's very best Christian authors...Wanda E. Brunstetter, Mary Connealy, Susan Page Davis, Cathy Marie Hake, and Joyce Livingston, to mention a few!

When you join Heartsong Presents, you'll enjoy four brand-new, mass-market, 176-page books—two contemporary and two historical—that will build you up in your faith when you discover God's role in every relationship you read about!

Mass Market 176 Pages

Imagine...four new romances every four weeks—with men and women like you who long to meet the one God has chosen as the love of their lives...all for the low price of $10.99 postpaid.

To join, simply visit www.heartsong presents.com or complete the coupon below and mail it to the address provided.

YES! Sign me up for Heartsong!

NEW MEMBERSHIPS WILL BE SHIPPED IMMEDIATELY!
Send no money now. We'll bill you only $10.99 postpaid with your first shipment of four books. Or for faster action, call 1-740-922-7280.

NAME _____

ADDRESS_____

CITY_____ STATE _____ ZIP _____

MAIL TO: HEARTSONG PRESENTS, P.O. Box 721, Uhrichsville, Ohio 44683
or sign up at WWW.HEARTSONGPRESENTS.COM